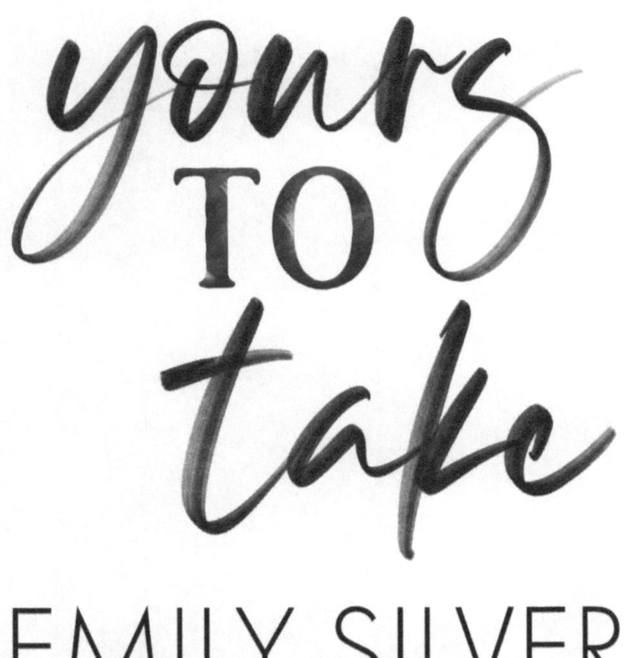

EMILY SILVER

TRAVELIN' HOOSIER BOOKS

To Tina Snider
Whom I love more than Cake Bake and Crumbl combined!

Chapter One

BLAKE

"This is crap, Blake."

The papers land on my desk with a thunk, startling me from the work at hand.

"Is that you saying that, or is it the studio heads saying that?"

I grab my latest draft and flip through the pages.

Clint drops into the chair across from my desk. With his salt-and-pepper hair and leathery skin, you'd think he was in his seventies. But being in the limelight aged him. As grumpy as my producer looks, he's never been one to beat around the bush with me.

Something I don't know if I appreciate right now.

"Both. Blake, this is the most uninspired story I think I've ever gotten from you."

"Way to hold back."

He throws his hands up in defense. "I'm sorry, do you want me to?"

"No," I mutter. "You could have been a bit nicer, though."

"Like those humans were to the zombies in this?" He points at the story on my desk.

Stacks upon stacks of ideas litter my crowded desk. The ideas have been there, but nothing that the studio wants to produce.

"I thought zombies were all the rage right now."

Clint shakes his head. "Aliens are in right now. People love blue creatures."

"So you're telling me I have to write a blue thing?"

"Not a blue thing, per se. But something that will hit like a blue creature. Me personally? I don't like it, but that's what is selling."

"I guess it's back to the drawing board."

An actual whiteboard hangs across one side of my small office at Malibu Studios. It's a small, boutique company that exploded onto the scenes years ago. I was able to get in on the ground level, probably with a little wheel greasing from my famous mother, but I've made my own name for myself. The Travers name will get you far in Hollywood.

Although, if you ask Clint, I'm going to crash and burn.

"What if I told you I had an idea for you?"

"I'm listening." I lean back in my chair, it squeaking as I go.

"While blue people are nice, people also want wholesome."

"You want me to give you wholesome aliens?"

He laughs. "No. The studio wants a family drama. We're seeing a resurgence in family life, and who better to pitch the idea than my best writer?"

"You don't need to butter me up."

"I'm not buttering you up. But Blake?"

"Yeah?"

"You need this idea to work. The studio is losing patience that they haven't gotten a marketable story from you in nine months."

"Don't remind me," I groan.

Ever since the success of my last TV show—a drama about a football team—I've been able to coast. With money flowing in, the studio was happy.

But once that last episode aired, the lead weight of pressure settled into my gut. Seven years of a hit TV show were gone.

"Get this to work, Blake. I don't want to fire you."

"Shit, really?"

He nods, picking up the knickknack on my desk and flicking it open. "Yes. You're a talented writer, and I know everyone has a rough patch, but the execs aren't happy."

"Jesus."

"So family drama. Get started."

He stands to leave. The silk scarf hangs around his neck. It's old-time, ostentatious Hollywood style.

"Wait. How long do I have?"

"The sooner the better, but more or less…three months."

"You expect me to come up with a show in three months when I've had nothing in the last nine?"

He reaches across my desk and pats me on the shoulder. "You're like the son I never had. I know you can do this. Don't make it weird and make me fire you."

"Yes, I'd hate for it to be fucking awkward for you." I roll my eyes at him.

"Three months." He holds up three fingers as he steps out of my office.

"Fuck."

I spear a hand through my hair and face out the

window—it's an incredible view of concrete buildings with the TV poster of my last hit.

The LA Pirates. A drama about the inner workings of a football team and their relationships. The studio ate it up. Critics loved it. Fans were cheering for it like they were their own team.

It was special. Something I wrote while watching football with friends one Sunday in a dive bar in LA.

And now, instead of coming up with my own idea, the studio is pushing an idea on me.

As if the pressure wasn't bad enough, I now have to work within a certain set of creative ideas. I hate being forced into a box. It never leads to good ideas.

The buzzing of my phone on my desk distracts me from my wayward thoughts.

Mom.

"Hey, Mom."

"Darling. I'm at the studio today and wanted you to meet me for lunch."

There's never an actual invitation from my mother. *I'm Tiffany Travers. They come to me,* she always says.

"I really don't have time today, Mom. I really need to get cracking on my next project."

"Nonsense. You can take thirty minutes to eat. Besides,"—there's a knock on my door—"I'm already here."

Shit.

I hang up the phone and walk over to her.

"Hi." I drop a peck on her perfectly made-up cheek. No matter where she is, no matter the time of day, she always has a full face of makeup on and wears the latest clothes from the top designers.

Today's feather jacket seems a touch out of place, but I've never been one to comment on what she wears. T-shirts and jeans cut it for me.

"Blake, dear. You're looking too thin. You really need to make time to eat."

Linking her arm with mine, Mom drags me out of my office. "I have a sandwich I can eat."

"That will not cut it. Besides, the new cafe opened and I hear everyone is buzzing about it."

As we make our way out of the office building that's centered on the studio lot, people gape at the woman on my arm.

Growing up, it was always weird to have a model/superstar for a mother. Everywhere we went, she was bombarded with people wanting to take a picture with her.

When you're a spitting image of her—brown hair and bright green eyes—people want a piece of you too.

"I only have thirty minutes."

"You really should make time for your mother."

Ironic that she tells me to make time for her now, when I was carted around by her when I was a kid and sent off with nannies while she worked.

"Excuse me, but do you mind if we step in front? We are on a time crunch."

"Oh, absolutely, Miss Travers."

My mother is also not beneath using her name to get ahead. Like beating the long column of workers standing in line for lunch break.

"We'll take two endive salads and sparkling waters."

"Mom, I can order for myself," I growl.

She ignores me. "Go find us a table."

I stalk off, like a toddler throwing a tantrum.

First Clint and now my mother. This isn't the best start to my day.

It's always been like this. My mother makes me absolutely crazy sometimes. Do I love her? Sure. About as much as anyone can when they hardly know them.

As much as I've made a name for myself, it still feels like I live in her shadow. And that I'll continue to live in her shadow for the rest of my life.

"The service here is incredible. Hardly had to wait at all." Mom walks up to the table, a haggard-looking worker following behind her with a tray.

"Thanks, man." I grab it from him and set it down before pulling out Mom's chair.

"Tell me about the projects you're working on."

Bangles clink on her arms as she opens her water and demurely sips from the bottle.

"Clint came by today to tell me I need to start working on a family drama."

"You?" Her face screws up. Or screws up as much as a woman with too much Botox can. "You don't have any idea about family drama. Clint really should just let you work."

I ignore her comment. Never mind the fact that she ran my dad off when I was little. "Doesn't matter. The exec's haven't been liking my ideas, so I need to come up with something. And fast."

"I'm sure you will, dear." She flicks her hand as if brushing away my concern, her rings flashing on her perfectly manicured hand. "I'll be off filming for the next few months."

And right back to her. Only took point-two seconds.

"Where are you off to this time?" I stuff an unsatisfying bite of salad into my mouth. Where my mother got the idea I like this stuff, I don't know.

"Japan. How exotic." Her eyes are wide with delight.

"I'm sure you'll have a great time."

Her phone buzzes from where it's sitting on the table. "Oh, I need to take this."

I lean back in my seat, frustrated. This is just like my mother. Inviting me to lunch because she says I need to spend more time with her and then picking up any call that comes in.

I try to get her attention, but she holds up a finger in a "give me a minute" sign. Clicking the plastic lid of my salad back into place, I stand.

"I have to go."

"Okay."

I don't even think she heard me.

Figures.

Not wanting to be wasteful, I take the sad, wilty salad back to my office and eat in peace.

If I could find any peace. The thought of getting fired is now sitting front and center in my mind. I've been with Malibu Studios since I was a lowly assistant, making coffee runs and printing more scripts than I knew what to do with.

I climbed my way up. All of my work has done well for the studio. It fucking sucks that after a few dry months, they can drop you faster than you can blink.

I can't be a writer if I have no studio to write for.

Chapter Two

BLAKE

"So, what are you going to do?" Eric throws a dart at the board in front of us.

"Pull a story out of my ass somehow."

"You know that doesn't work." He points at me with the next dart in his hand.

"It's either that or get fired and then spend the next five years trying to find work. And when I don't, I'll have to move back in with my mom, and that's the last thing I want to do."

Eric shudders. "I could not imagine moving back in with my mom at twenty-seven."

"You still live with your mom."

"Ass. She lives with me. House is in my name."

One of the few friends I have here, Eric and I met on his first day as a director's assistant for my football show. He's made a killing for himself and is now at the helm of his own show. One filled to the brim with blue creatures.

For someone so well-known, he's not easily picked out in a crowd. His trademark long, blond hair is pulled back under a hat. It hides the scar that slices down his face. Some childhood accident he won't tell me about.

"You're so easy to rile up," I say with a grin as he steps away from the line and I take my shot with the darts.

"You're dodging my question." Eric sips his beer.

"Clint tells me they don't want zombies, but aliens are in, then hands me a family drama. Why can't I have a family of aliens?"

"People only like aliens if they're having sex."

"Dude." I throw my arms out wide. "I really don't want to be discussing alien sex right now."

"You're the one that brought aliens up."

"Regardless,"—I eye him before turning my focus back to the round, checkered board—"what family drama hasn't been done?"

"What about a family in Antarctica?"

"I don't want to shoot in the cold for the next eight years. Next." I throw my last dart before going to collect them. "Fifty-seven points."

"You win. I'm done." He hands me my beer.

"No need to be such a sore loser." I smile around the glass as I sip on the hoppy goodness.

"I'm not a sore loser. I just hate playing darts with you."

"Means you're a sore loser, Eric."

"At least my job isn't on the line." He gives me a smarmy grin.

"Dick."

"After I've spent all night trying to help you. Tsk tsk."

"You have given me exactly one idea." I hold up a finger to him.

"What about one set in the West?"

"Like *Little House on the Prairie*?" I give him a questioning look.

"Do you want to be fired? Because it sounds like you do."

"I don't want to do something that's already been done."

"Hear me out." He rests his arm on the high-top table and leans across. "You see all these family shows set in bigger cities, but none that are in small, western towns. It doesn't need to be anything over-the-top, but I'm sure you can find some inspiration."

I weigh the idea. "Not a terrible plan."

"Here." Eric pulls out his phone, taps a few buttons, and shoves it in my face. "Look at that. Five-star ranches you can stay at."

Dixon Creek Ranch.

With a sprawling property, cabins, and mountain views, it looks like it's straight from a Hollywood set.

"Maybe it'll be good for me to get away for a little bit."

"I think all the sun is getting to your head."

I subtly flip him off, scratching the side of my face with my middle finger. "I've lived here most of my life."

"Which means you need to get out. Take a few weeks and get some fresh air. That beach bungalow isn't doing you any good, filled with all those trophies from your mom."

It's true. To buy anything in this area would've cost me my firstborn. Instead, my mom sacrificed her beach bungalow—her words, not mine—for me. As long as I didn't touch her precious trophy room.

I rarely go in there. Her successes are suffocating on the best of days, let alone when I've hit a block.

"This might be the smallest town I've ever seen." I flip through pictures on the website. A small town with maybe one stoplight, it looks like it's pure Americana.

"Which means it'd be the perfect place for you to escape to. No one would know who you are."

"I mean, look at these cabins." I show Eric the private escapes on the property. With nothing nearby, it really would be the writing retreat I need.

"I hope it comes with indoor plumbing. You wouldn't survive living in the Old West."

"You're a dick."

"You make it too easy," he bellows.

"You wait and see." I slide his phone back over to him and pour myself another beer from the pitcher. "Clint is going to love this pitch, and then when he's looking for directors, I'm going to skip right over you."

"Please. You love me." He dismisses my words.

"Or maybe I'll just direct it myself."

"Now who's being a dick?"

I laugh at him and top off his drink. "Takes one to know one."

"If you didn't give me my big break, I don't think I'd keep you around."

"And if I didn't like you so much, I'd drop you."

Eric really is family to me. We clicked on day one. He's one of the few real people in this business. It makes being around him easy.

Very few people want to get to know the real me. They either see me as their meal ticket or use me to get to my mom.

I hate how fake this business can be.

"Million dollar question. What are you going to do?"

I hold my glass up in cheers.

"Guess I'm going to Dixon."

Chapter Three

GEMMA

"Hi. Welcome to Dixon Creek Ranch. We're so happy to have you here."

"Oh my gosh. This place is absolutely marvelous."

"Thank you. We pride ourselves on being the premier destination this side of the Tetons."

The grin on my face is warm and welcoming. It's a real smile today, but something I've had to perfect over the years even when dealing with terrible guests.

"Will we get to play with the buffalo?" a little voice squeaks from below the counter.

"They're really big, and you don't want to mess with their horns. But I'm sure I can find a stuffed one for you," I tell the little boy.

"Really?" His eyes light up. It's already waiting for him in their cabin, so I know he's going to love it.

"Absolutely. Now, let's get you checked in so you can start your western adventure."

As I check in our newest guests, I can see their eyes roaming over the lobby of the main lodge.

It's changed over the years, becoming the jewel it is

today. Two-story windows look out over the Tetons. Over-sized furniture faces a large stone hearth that, on late wintry days like today, holds a crackling fire to lure our guests inside. Red-and-black-plaid wallpaper makes it warm and welcoming.

"You're going to be in the Idaho cabin. Just head out these doors, and our bellman will walk over with you. And if you need anything, just call."

"Thank you."

"Enjoy your stay."

"Hey Gemma!" a voice carries from the other side of the bar. Behind me, the lobby opens up into the main restaurant and bar where guests can get anything they need at any time.

"What is it, Peter?"

"I thought you said you needed more potato vodka?"

Dropping the "be back soon" sign on the front desk, I follow my brother's voice behind the bar.

"We do. We're down to one bottle."

"Then why does the order say fifteen bottles?"

"I don't know. I don't run the show, so I didn't place the order." I grab the clipboard from him. "Did you really bring that many?"

"I figured you might have had an event or something."

"You would know if we had something planned at the ranch."

I shake my head at my older brother.

"Do you want me to leave the extras?"

"No. We don't go through them that quickly. You'll burn through them at the bar."

Peter owns and runs one of the top potato vodka distilleries in Idaho. Having started it when he was twenty, it's one of Dixon's most well-known attractions. People love sampling his vodka at his bar, The Tipsy Cocktail.

"I'll take some over to Gramps's house for family dinner this week. You planning on coming?" he asks as he hefts a box of clattering bottles back onto the bar.

"If I can get my shift covered for me."

"You're her boss. Tell her to cover for you."

I quirk a brow in his direction. "Still not the boss, Peter."

"Why haven't you talked to Gramps about that?" He crosses his arms, leaning back against the bar. It's always quiet at the ranch this time of year. That weird in-between time of winter and spring where the weather can't make up it's mind. A little snow today, then tomorrow a spring storm that will bring with it the hot weather I love.

"You know why."

"Logan is doing okay right now. His next surgery isn't for another couple of weeks."

"I know, but I don't want anything to distract from his recovery."

"Seriously, I thought the baby of the family was supposed to need more attention."

I laugh at that. "You've always been the drama queen of the family."

"Hey!" He shoves at my shoulder. "I am not. That's always been Logan."

"Whatever you say, Peter."

"Listen, I need to get back to the bar. We have a new band coming in tonight, and they're all the rage."

"Oh, you mean the Flying Toaster Time Machine?"

"Jesus. Is that really their name?"

I laugh. "Dwight said they were being creative when they named themselves."

"Dwight, as in Layla's high school boyfriend, Dwight?"

"Yes. Didn't you know that when you booked them?"

"No. Nash has taken over the booking of all entertainment." Peter gets a lopsided grin on his face, thinking about his partner.

The two of them were high school sweethearts, or whatever the summer equivalent is. But Nash left, leaving Peter heartbroken.

Fast forward seven years, and Nash is now living with Peter in his cabin on the property.

"Go run your bar, and I'll see you at dinner this week."

"See ya, Gem." Peter drops a kiss on my head before leaving.

There are a few guests mingling, but with it being early spring, it's not quite busy season.

These are the times I love my job. I love the quiet before summer starts. Meeting and chatting with guests is my favorite part of this job. Even if I wasn't born to work here, I'd still want to.

Dixon Creek Ranch has been in the family for as long as I can remember. My grandparents ran it until they retired, and then my parents took over. When my mom and dad decided they wanted to retire early, I was barely old enough to work the front desk.

But I came to work and haven't looked back since. I love everything about this place.

The only downside? I'm still just a front desk clerk. Sure, I know more about this place than anyone else, but I haven't moved up. It's something Gramps never wants to discuss with me. I don't know why.

It's not like there are many options for me if I wanted to find another job. Dixon is twenty minutes away, and with a population of three thousand, it makes jobs scarce.

It also makes dating hard. Really, really hard.

I've either known everyone since kindergarten, or they're tourists who blow through town treating it like shit under their shoe.

Probably why I still have my V-card. No one worth giving it up to.

Regardless, I wouldn't trade my life for anything. This small town is in my blood. Dixon raised me, and I wouldn't want to be anywhere else.

Chapter Four

GEMMA

"I'm going to be okay, right?"

I tighten the helmet strap on our youngest rider today.

"Absolutely. Buttercup is our best horse, and Billy here will make sure you have the best time."

"Okay." The little girl smiles brightly up at me before I help her up onto the horse.

This is one of my favorite parts of my job. I love getting to help people overcome their fears.

But based on how she's cooing at Buttercup, she's going to be just fine.

"Want to muck out the stalls while we're gone?" Billy shouts back at me as they head out.

"Only have thirty other things to do today, so why not?" I laugh.

"Thanks, Gemma."

I shake my head. Mucking out the stalls isn't my favorite thing to do, but I'll never say no to pitching in and helping.

Popping in my earbuds, I get to work. I try to help out

when I can, but most of the time, my days are spent working inside.

Finding the wheelbarrow, I head to the first empty stall. This time of day, all the horses are out in the pasture. It's starting to warm up after the last wintry weather blew through.

The work is easy enough, but as the day goes on, it starts getting warmer in the barn. By the time I get to the last stall, I'm not paying much attention as I push the wheelbarrow out of the stall.

Right into someone passing by.

My arms are tired, and I can't steady the ominous tilt to the wheelbarrow before it goes spilling over. Right onto the person I crashed into. I rip my earbuds out, fire heating my cheeks.

I can't believe I did that.

"Oh my God! I'm so sorry!"

"Umm, what's on me?" The voice is silky smooth as I look at the person I bumped into.

I just dumped a wheelbarrow full of horse shit on quite possibly the hottest man I've ever met.

Kill me now.

"Oh God. I am so sorry!"

My face flushes even hotter when his green eyes connect with mine. It sends a chill racing through my body.

They're the same color as the pine trees that cover our property. With short brown hair and a dimple that cuts his cheek, he's sexy without even having to try.

"It's okay."

"No, it's not." I pull the gloves off my hands, trying to think of a way to make this right. "I can't believe I ran into you."

"I promise, it's fine. I was trying to get the lay of the land since I'll be here for the next few weeks."

Even better—he's a new guest.

Great first impression I made. I smack my hand against my head. Sweat and flyaway hairs stick to my forehead.

"Could we at least dry clean your pants for you?"

"You trying to get me out of my pants?" He crosses his arms, staring down at me. An easy smile graces his face.

Is it too much for me to hope for a sinkhole to swallow me right now?

"No! I'm just trying to make this better."

The mysterious guest rests both of his hands on my shoulders. What's meant to be calming sets me even more on edge.

Not because it's unwelcome, but because of the reaction it fires in me. The heat sitting in my cheeks spreads everywhere. It even makes my toes curl from his firm touch.

"While I will probably take you up on the laundry, I promise you, this is fine. I've been in worse situations."

"Worse than having horse shit dumped on you?"

He laughs, and it does nothing to the butterflies that are threatening to explode out of me.

"Well, no. I'm trying to make you feel better."

"Ugh." I slap both hands over my eyes. Maybe if I wish for him to disappear, he will. But when I peek one eye open? He's still here—still smiling at me as if this is how he spends an afternoon.

"I take it it's not working?"

"No. I'm going to go bury myself out in the field." I throw a thumb over my shoulder.

"No, you're not." He grabs my arm as I go to spin around. "It was an accident."

"I think you severely underestimate how embarrassing this is for me."

"Want me to dump horse shit on you to make you feel better?" he asks.

"If it would make you feel better, then yes."

He shakes his head. "Not really."

I shrug a shoulder. "Besides, it probably wouldn't help since it's already all over my boots."

"Horse shit?" he asks.

"Can we please stop saying that?"

I'm mortified. I can't believe I'm even standing here having this conversation. I pay more attention when I'm mucking the stalls. Seeing as how it's Sunday, it's quiet and no one is around. I thought I had the place to myself.

"You're right." He holds out his hand. "I'm Blake."

"Gemma Winchester." I take his hand. Electricity zings through my arm. "You're staying over in the Tetons cabin."

"Should I be worried you know which cabin I'm in?" He raises a brow at me, and I realize my hand is still connected to his.

"And now I'm going to go bury myself in the field. It was nice to meet you. Please tell my family I love them."

He barks out a laugh at me, dropping my hand. "Need some company?"

"To meet my demise?" I shake my head. "I think I can manage."

Blake gives me a small smile. That little dimple of his pops out again. "Pity. I was hoping to have a guide for the rest of my afternoon."

That perks my ears up. "You mean no one showed you the grounds?"

He gives a casual shrug. "No. I didn't take them up on it. I wanted to explore on my own."

"Note to self—don't let the guests decline the tours, otherwise they'll end up in covered in crap."

He holds his arms out wide. "So you work here then?"

I point to the wheelbarrow that's still on its side. "What gave it away?"

"Right." Blake's laugh is awkward. "Seems pretty obvious now that I say it."

"I'm glad you think so." My laugh is nervous. "I probably should get going. Finish out the last of the stalls before the group comes back."

"You want help?"

"God, no!" Based on his reaction, my face must show my shock. "I mean, no. You're a guest. I can manage."

"Thank you for not taking me up on that." He rubs a finger over his eyebrow. He looks slightly nervous, which makes my nerves quiet down.

"Then why did you offer?" I smile at him.

"Seemed like the polite thing to do. I honestly have no idea what I'd be doing."

"We save that for your second visit to the ranch."

Shoving his hands in his pockets, he takes a step back. "I guess that means I'll have to come back for a return visit."

Oh, I wish he would.

"It was nice to meet you, Blake. If you need anything, I'm usually in the lobby."

"It was nice to meet you, Gemma." Blake smiles at me. It's dazzling. It wouldn't surprise me if I had sparks shooting out of my ears. "Horse shit and all."

Chapter Five

BLAKE

Damn. This place is pretty incredible. The pictures Eric and I looked at didn't do it justice.

Kicking my feet up on the railing, I rock back in the chair on the porch of my cabin. The mountains are spread out in front of me. Buds are popping up on the trees, signaling the start of spring.

The quiet of the cabins back here should be the perfect setting for me to start writing. Yet, nothing.

Not one single usable word. It's like my brain has stalled out on how to write a scene that would translate to TV.

My cell vibrates in my pocket. Pulling it out, it's not exactly the person I want to talk to right now. But, I know it'll be worse if I don't answer.

"Clint. How's it going?"

"How are things out in Montana?" Clint asks by way of greeting.

"Idaho."

"Does it matter? All some random place that isn't LA."

I laugh. It's just like Clint to think that LA is the center of the universe.

"It's going."

"What does that mean?"

I scrub a hand over my forehead. "I'm not writing if that's what you're asking."

Clint scoffs over the phone. "Do I need to come out there and force you to write? Too many distractions out there for you."

"And you think this isn't a distraction?" The more pressure Clint puts on me, the harder it's going to be to get anything done.

"Do you really think you're going to find inspiration wherever you are?" Clint's voice is skeptical.

"Dixon, Clint. At least know where I am."

A few guests wander back to their cabin next to me, talking excitedly about their day. Something about fishing.

"I'll learn it if you start making me the big bucks from it."

"Now you sound like my mother."

"Hey, I have to think about the big picture. You just worry about putting pen to paper."

An older woman, carrying a large dish, is now walking up the path. Straight to my cabin.

"Listen, Clint, I have to go."

"Words. Give me words."

I hang up the phone and stand. The older woman walks up the steps, a smile painted on her face.

"Hi." I try to hide the confusion in my voice, but I must not do a good job of it.

"Is that how you welcome someone to your home? Your momma must not have taught you right."

"That's a conversation for another day." I give her my biggest smile, trying to steer the conversation away from the topic of my mother. That will do nothing to help me start writing.

"I heard you were going to be staying around these parts awhile and I wanted to welcome you to town." Her smile brightens even more.

"I am." I extend my hand to her. "Blake Travers."

"Oh, like the famous movie star?" she asks, shifting the dish to her left hand and shaking mine.

Of course this woman would recognize the name.

"That's my mother." I can't fight the grimace on my face.

"Well, with a face like that, I bet you're in the movies too."

"Not quite. I write them."

"That's fascinating." She shifts the pie dish she's holding from one hand to the other. "Are you going to make a little old lady stand out here all day, or will you invite me in?"

"Shit, sorry." I grab the dish from her hand and push open the door to the cabin.

"Not a worry, darling." She pats me on the face as she walks inside. "Maybe we can share a slice."

"Only if you introduce yourself to me."

"Heavens." She pats her graying hair down. "Here I am criticizing your manners, but I haven't introduced myself. Mrs. Phillips. I make the best pie in town."

"You do?"

She points her finger at me. "Don't let anyone here tell you otherwise."

"Okay." Grabbing two plates from the open shelf, I take a knife off the counter and slice into the blueberry pie. "Is there someone else I need to watch out for?"

I hand her a slice. She takes it eagerly.

"That Mrs. Reynolds will try to push her pie on you. Just know I delivered mine first."

I take a large bite, trying not to get in the middle of a pie debate. Except, this pie is pretty damn delectable.

Mrs. Phillips points her fork at me. "See? You like it."

"I don't think I've ever tasted anything so delicious."

Her smile is smug. "Like I said, best pie in all of Dixon."

"I appreciate you stopping by. How'd you know I was even here?"

"I know everything that happens in Dixon."

"I don't doubt that." I shovel another forkful in my mouth.

"Has the town been welcoming?"

It doesn't surprise me that this woman is the one here dropping off a pie. Even though she recognized the Travers name, she couldn't care less as to who I am.

Quite the change from being wanted for that name alone.

"I haven't ventured in yet. But everyone here at the ranch has been great."

She smiles, taking her own small bite. "Gemma runs a tight ship around here."

"I've had the pleasure of meeting her."

"You have, have you?"

There's a tone to her voice. One I'm not sure if I should like.

"She was very welcoming." I don't tell her that it involved dumping shit all over me—she doesn't need to know that.

"Good. She's a peach, that one."

Mrs. Phillips's eyes are sparkling. The last thing I need is her getting any ideas. My time here is about one thing and one thing only. I don't need any distractions.

"Listen, I should probably get back to work."

She brushes her hands off on her pant legs. "You make sure you finish that pie."

"How can I get your dish back to you?"

"Give it to Gemma. She'll make sure it gets back to me." She winks at me as she heads out the door.

Great. I haven't been in town for a week, and this woman is already trying to push Gemma on me.

The last thing I expected when I rolled into town was an old bitty stopping by. I should've known.

A town this small would've known I'd be arriving. And make a point to welcome me.

Now, instead of focusing on my new show, I have to worry about dodging the old women in Dixon.

And not think about the girl who crashed into me.

No matter how sexy I think she is.

Chapter Six

GEMMA

"I really appreciate this, Gem."

"It's no big deal, Mason. It's quiet today." The lobby is empty except for the one person who I want to see, but also don't want to see.

"Willow, you'll be good for Aunt Gemma, right?"

She nods. "Of course, Daddy."

"Mason. I'm serious. Call Ivy. I know she's looking for something before her job starts this fall."

My grump of a big brother shakes his head at me. "I don't want to inconvenience her."

"But you'll inconvenience me?" I cross my arms, mirroring his stern look.

"You said this wasn't a big deal."

"It's not. But you need to find someone to stay with her since you're taking on more hours at the bar."

Mason scrubs a hand down his face. Out of all my siblings, I look the most like Mason. Except with fewer frown lines. Same brown hair. Same brown eyes. Just ten years between us.

"Send me her number."

"Promise you'll call her."

"Just send me her number," Mason grumbles.

"Aunt Gemma! Can we shoot arrows today?" Willow tugs on my shirt.

"Of course."

"I gotta go, Pipsqueak. Have a good time with Aunt Gem." Mason drops down and wraps his arms around his daughter.

"Love you, Daddy."

"Love you." He turns his attention to me. "I owe you."

"It's fine. Willow and I are going to have a great afternoon."

Mason drops a kiss on my cheek and rushes out the door. His daughter has now moved to the corner of the lobby, where she's talking to our latest guest.

"What are you writing?" Willow is leaning up on the desk, brown curls bouncing as she peers around the computer screen.

"It's going to be a TV show."

"Willow, leave Blake alone." I grab Willow by the shoulders, steering her away from the desk. "He's busy."

"She's not bothering me. I'm not getting much done." Blake smiles as he shuts his laptop lid.

"What kind of TV show?" Willow asks him, ignoring me.

"Well, it's supposed to be about a family, but I'm not doing a good job of it."

"Do you have a family?" Willow asks.

Blake smiles at her. "I do. But they're not here."

"You don't have anyone to play with?"

"I'm here to work."

"Work is boring." Willow screws her face up. "You should come play with us."

"Oh yeah?" Blake looks up at me. "Is that okay with your Aunt Gemma?"

I swallow, my face getting hot. All I keep thinking about is running smack into him after mucking out the stalls.

"Of course it is." Willow elbows me in the leg. "We're going to shoot arrows."

"That sounds like fun."

"You really don't have to come," I say, giving him an out. "I don't want to distract you."

Blake rises, towering above me. His presence is overwhelming. It didn't feel this way the other day. Probably because I doused him in horse shit and had never been more embarrassed in my life.

Now? Every cell is tingling with awareness.

"I need the distraction. I'm pretty sure I've only written five words. *Insert clever thing here.*"

"That's only four words," Willow pipes up.

Blake bursts out laughing. "You're right."

"C'mon, Aunt Gemma. Let him come shoot arrows. I bet I'm better than him."

"Willow!"

"She's right." Blake has an easy smile on his face. "I don't think I've ever shot a bow and arrow before."

"Well then." I grab Willow's hand. "I think we'll need to show you how."

"Yes!" Willow runs off ahead of us, knowing exactly where to go.

"That's your niece?" Blake holds the back door open for me.

"It is."

"She's feisty."

"I don't know what gets into her."

"She must get it from you." Blake winks at me.

"Just shoot me with an arrow," I groan.

"I might. I've never done this before."

"Aunt Gemma is a good teacher!" Willow chirps. She's vibrating with excitement. This is one of her favorite things when coming out to the ranch.

The archery range is a small clearing near the pasture. Far enough away to not cause any scares to the animals. There's a fair distance between the targets and the line. Willow has a bow for each of us.

"Okay. How do we do this?" Blake takes the bow from Willow.

"You knock it, aim, and then shoot," Willow tells him.

"That's it?"

Willow's answer is showing him how it's done, including firing a bullseye. Girl knows how to shoot.

"Damn,"—Blake whistles—"I don't know if I'll be able to do that."

"Watch me, then you can try it, then I'll help if you need it." I give him an encouraging smile. Knocking my own arrow, I step up to the line.

I can feel Blake's watchful eyes on me as I step into position. I could do this in my sleep, but I want to impress him. Setting my feet, I pull the bow up and anchor my hand before aiming and firing.

Dead center in the ring.

"Wow. You're both scary good at this."

Willow is beaming as she shoots another arrow.

"You try. I promise it's not as hard as it looks."

"I don't know about that." Blake's movements are awkward. Willow comes to stand next to me as we watch him.

"Want to bet that I can get a bullseye?" Blake asks her.

"Daddy usually asks me that when he thinks I think he can't do something but actually can."

Willow has never met a stranger, and Blake takes it all in stride. "I don't know how good I am. But if I don't get a bullseye, I'll buy you a sundae back at the ranch."

Willow's eyes light up. "Okay!"

"You think I can get a bullseye?" Blake asks me.

"It's that center thing, in case you're wondering where to aim." I snicker.

"Wow. No one has any confidence in me. I'll prove you both wrong."

Blake sets his feet, takes aim, and fires. The arrow hits the ground a few feet in front of the target. Willow's giggling next to me as she runs to collect the arrows.

"Damn. I at least thought I'd hit the target."

"Everyone has to start somewhere." I grab an arrow from the quiver and step up next to Blake. He smells like cinnamon. It reminds me of Christmas morning.

"You notched the arrow right,"—I grab his hand—"but your stance was off. May I?"

Blake nods. Standing next to him, I mimic the move for shooting and help him into position.

It's hard being this close to him. His muscles are hard under my hands. I want to feel every inch of him.

It's been a long time since I've felt anything like this for another person. There's not even been a brief stirring of something like interest. All the guys I dated over the years were mediocre at best. After my high school boyfriend turned out to be a cheating ass, it made me wary of new guys.

There's something about Blake that sucked me in from the minute I first ran into him. *Literally*.

I shouldn't be so taken with him. He's a guest. Guests always leave.

"Is this better?" Blake asks. His voice is barely above a

whisper. It sends shockwaves through me. How can one man's voice be so delicious?

"Yes." My own voice sounds gravelly to my ears. I step back, taking a breath of Blake-free air. "Pull back, hold for a second, and then release."

This time, Blake lands it on the target. Not anywhere close to the bullseye, but he made it on.

"Hey!" A huge smile greets me when I look at him. "That was pretty badass!"

"That was great!"

"Aunt Gemma is a really good teacher!" Willow chimes in. "She taught me!"

"No wonder you're so good." Blake ruffles her hair. "Maybe she'll give me some private lessons."

The wink Blake sends my way has my cheeks flushing again.

Is there a limit to how many times one can blush in front of the same man? Because I'm pretty sure I've rocketed right past it.

"Only for my favorite guests."

"Something to strive toward, I guess."

"Since you didn't get the bullseye, does that mean I get a sundae?"

"It sure does."

"Can we have it now?" Willow turns hopeful eyes on me.

"Don't you want to shoot some more?"

"I want to make a sundae with Blake."

"Only if your aunt says it's okay," Blake tells her.

"I guess it's okay."

"Yes!" Willow takes off toward the main lodge, a blur of dust kicking up behind her.

"She's pretty great," Blake tells me. "How old is she?"

"Seven going on seventeen. She thinks she runs the show around here."

"Giving you a run for your money then?"

"Me? I'm just a lowly front desk employee."

"Really?" Blake raises a brow as we follow in Willow's wake.

"There have always been other people in charge until now. But with my brother needing more help and attention, it's kind of fallen to the wayside."

"What happened to your brother?"

"He got injured playing football. He got septic in the hospital, but thankfully he's okay now. It's taken a lot of surgeries to repair his leg, so it's a new normal for all of us."

"Wow, I'm sorry to hear that, Gemma."

I'm not one to talk about things like this with virtual strangers. Something about Blake makes it easy to open up to him.

"He's okay, so that's all that matters."

"You plan on staying around here then?" Blake stuffs his hands into his pockets as we hit the porch.

I nod. "Dixon is my home. There's no other place in the world I could imagine living."

"It does have a certain charm to it."

I laugh. "I take it you haven't been into town yet?"

"Not yet, no."

"You don't want to miss out on it. Dixonites are quite the townspeople."

"Maybe you could give me the grand tour?"

"Sure. I'd like that." I don't even hesitate. I want to spent more time with this man.

"Me too."

Blake and I are standing on the porch, neither one of us quite knowing what to do. I want to draw this out, spend more time with him. Turns out, I'm not the only one.

Willow bursts outside. "Oh my God! Aunt Gemma! C'mon, I want to make sundaes!"

Grabbing Blake's hand, Willow drags him inside.

"You coming with? I might need help with my sprinkles." The corners of Blake's lips quirk up.

"Only to help with the sprinkles."

I follow after the two of them.

I guess I'm not the only Winchester taken with Blake. And I can't decide if that's a good thing or a bad thing.

I'll have to settle for sundaes until then.

Chapter Seven

The blinking cursor on my screen mocks me. It's like my computer knows I need to be writing, but nothing will draw the ideas out of me.

Fucking studio. They think by telling me my job is on the line, it'll help the ideas come. Instead, I'm handed an idea that I need to make work about a family drama.

No pressure or anything.

"How's it going?"

Gemma pops up at the desk beside me.

"If you can write a story for me, that'd be great." I gesture a hand at my laptop.

"That bad, huh?"

"Yeah." I slam the lid. The main lodge, while quiet at this time of day, has filled with people. People usually have me brimming with ideas, but today, nothing.

Gemma stares down at me, like she's contemplating something. "Do you have time this afternoon?"

"For what?"

"The weather is going to be great this afternoon, so maybe a hike will help clear your head."

"How about now?"

"Oh. I mean, now works too."

I stand. "I will get nowhere sitting here spinning my wheels, so why not? Maybe it'll jump-start something in my brain."

Gemma smiles at me. A real, not-fake-at-all, wrinkles-around-your-eyes smile. Something I'm not used to seeing in Hollywood. "You can fill me in on your process, too. Meet me back here in ten minutes and we'll head out."

She spins on her heel, heading out of the lobby. Her long hair swings down her back as her hips sway with each step.

I shouldn't be as taken with her as I am, but I can't help it. The last time this happened, I got screwed over. Another person used me to get a leg up in Hollywood.

Not the first time, but definitely the last time.

Heading back to my cabin, I drop off my laptop and change into the most appropriate clothes I have for hiking.

I didn't really pack for outdoor activities, but thankfully I had the foresight to pack boots. Grabbing a water bottle from the fridge, I walk back over to the main lodge to meet Gemma.

It's hard to believe her family owns all of this land. Acres as far as the eye can see—and then some. The main lodge is incredible. A log mansion wouldn't quite be the correct term. While it has some guest rooms inside, the lobby and restaurant are the main jewels.

The tall windows let in the morning sun as a fire crackles in the fireplace, warding off the early spring chill. It's western chic, if that's considered a thing.

"You ready?"

Gemma is waiting for me in one of the rocking chairs on the back deck.

With a plaid shirt hanging open over a Dixon Bar and

Grill tee, worn-in hiking boots, plus a backpack sitting by her feet, she looks like Annie Oakley.

"You're a regular modern-day country girl."

She laughs, bright and loud. "I don't think that's how anyone would describe me."

"Well, you already know more than I do."

She looks me over, noticing the water bottle in my hand. "Is that all you're bringing?"

"What? Water's important."

Gemma shakes her head, strands of hair falling loose around her face. "At least you got that fact right, Hollywood."

"Hey, I resent that." I point a finger at her. "I just didn't plan on having time to go hiking."

"I'll carry it for you, and if you need anything, I packed a few snacks."

"Great."

Gemma sets off through the cabins to a trail marker.

"How hard do you want to go today?"

"Meaning…" I quirk a brow in her direction, my mind instantly going to all the hard things I want to do with her.

"Miles. Long, short, easy, hard? We have options."

There's a map that shows the trails leading out of the ranch to the mountains. "Medium?"

"I have just the trail for you. It'll give us magnificent views of the Tetons." She squeezes my bicep, sending a jolt of heat straight through me.

Shit. That's something new.

Not that it's entirely unwelcome, but it's not the reason that I'm here. Work is my sole focus. If I lose my job, it's going to be hard to find another studio to pick up a writer with writer's block.

It takes me a minute to realize Gemma has taken off without me, so I jog to catch up.

"How long have you lived here?" I ask as she guides me through the woods.

"I've lived here my entire life."

"Really?"

Gemma holds a tree branch out of the way and motions for me to pass her.

"I love it here. Why would I leave?"

"I guess that's fair."

"Have you always lived in LA?"

I stop at the fork in the trail and let her pass me to take the lead.

"No. I lived in Paris with my mom for a few years before we moved to LA. She had a modeling career when I was little before she became an actress."

"Wow, Paris? That sounds like a fun place to grow up."

Gemma takes a turn, and the incline of the hill gets a little steeper.

"It was, and it wasn't. My mom was always working, so I was with nannies most of the time. The ones I liked would take me on adventures, but others just stayed at home with me."

Stopping, Gemma turns to me with a sad look on her face. "That sounds lonely."

"It was." I'm not going to lie to her. "But once we moved back to the states and I started school, it was easy enough to make friends."

"And no brothers and sisters?"

The trail widens up ahead and I fall into step once again beside her.

"Just me."

"Wow. I can't imagine life without my brothers and sisters."

"How many do you have?"

"There's five of us."

"I can't even begin to imagine growing up with that many people in the house." I laugh.

"You're telling me. And I'm the baby."

"I'm guessing you got away with a lot growing up."

Her smile is contagious. It's the one that I can imagine working on everyone she knows to get what she wants.

"I did. It drove my older sister, Layla, crazy. She was always in trouble for breaking curfew with her boyfriend."

"You didn't get in trouble?"

The trail gets darker as we head farther into a copse of trees.

She shakes her head. "All my friends had curfews, so I never had the chance to break it. Dixon is a small town. If you were going to be home late, your parents knew before you even had the chance to tell them."

"I don't know if I'd like being the center of gossip."

"Oh, you are."

"Wait, I am?" I hold out an arm, stopping her.

"Of course you are. The hotshot writer from LA? You were the talk of the town at the farmers' market this past weekend."

"What were they saying?"

Gemma digs in her backpack and hands me my water. I take it, gulping down a few cool sips.

"Ghost Pepper Dick wanted to know if you were going to make us all sound like hillbillies when you write us into your show."

I nearly spit out my water. "I'm sorry. Ghost Pepper Dick?"

She looks at me like I'm crazy. "Ghost Pepper Dick. He grows peppers and makes hot sauce. He's been doing it since I was little, and that's what Peter called him."

"Well, you can tell Ghost Pepper Dick that he'll be in my series, and I won't make him sound like a hillbilly."

"He gets to be in it? Does that mean I get to be in it too?"

I hand the water bottle back to Gemma. Lifting the bottom of my shirt, I wipe the sweat from my brow.

I don't miss the way her eyes track over my stomach.

"If you want to be."

Her eyes snap back up to mine, a blush blooming in her cheeks that wasn't there before.

"Who do you think would play me?" Her smile is glowing as we head farther up the mountain.

"That's a loaded question."

"How is that a loaded question?"

The trail veers left, and I follow her. Being this close to her, I have an indecent view of her ass and the way her leggings are perfectly hugging it as she moves up the trail.

Fuck. I do not need to be getting hard out here with her.

"It's a loaded question because what if you don't like who I pick to play you? I need to get to know you more."

"Okay, then let's get to know one another."

Gemma and I fire questions back and forth at one another. It helps distract from the upward winding of the trail. My legs are on fire from muscles I never knew I had getting a workout.

Before I know it, the trail leads to a flat clearing.

The trees are sparser here, the first signs of life starting to peek through. The valley below extends out from the mountains behind us. The ranch looks like tiny specks from up here. Dixon looks even smaller from this high up.

"Holy shit."

"Pretty incredible, right?"

Gemma is beaming next to me. Her cheeks are pink from the hike up.

"Definitely beats the views back home."

Dropping onto a broken log, Gemma sits and riffles through her bag. I take the spot next to her, kicking out my tired legs.

"This is one of my favorite spots."

"I can see why. It's pretty great."

So great, in fact, that the familiar spark of an idea is taking hold in my head. When the studio gave me the idea of creating a family drama, I didn't have a clue as to what I was supposed to be writing.

Sitting here with Gemma? I'm starting to get some. It's making my fingers itch to get back to my keyboard so I don't lose any of them.

"If you could live anywhere besides LA, where would it be?"

"Honestly? I've never really thought of living anywhere else. It'd be hard to be a screenwriter and not be in LA. Maybe NYC?"

"One coast to the next? I wouldn't last in NYC."

"Why not?"

"There's way too many people there for my liking. I'm quite happy with Dixon."

I nudge her knee with my elbow. "I think you're going to need to take me into town. I want to meet all these people that are gossiping about my presence."

"Mrs. Phillips and Mrs. Reynolds will fight like teenage girls over you."

"Mrs. Phillips seemed nice when I met her."

"You've already met her?" Gemma pops a pretzel into her mouth.

"I did. And she knew exactly who I was and who I was related to."

Gemma slaps a hand over her face. "Oh God. I'm so sorry. Sometimes she can't control what comes out of her mouth."

"It's fine. I don't think she meant anything by it. I've got a good sense of people at this point in my life."

"That sounds sad."

I shake my head. "Not when you're used to being used by people wanting to land a certain part."

Growing up with a model-turned-actress, everyone wanted a piece of me. It's why my true friendships are few and far between.

"I'm sorry." Gemma's eyes are on me. "That must've been hard."

I shrug a shoulder. "After my first girlfriend treated me like shit because I wouldn't help her get a part, I know what to look for."

Gemma winces. "She used you for a part?"

I nod. "Comes with the territory, I guess."

"Still. I'm sorry that happened to you. I don't know if I could deal with that."

"Trust me, I didn't either. Not when your first kiss, hell your first time, is plastered all over the tabloids in a tell-all story."

Her cheeks grow even more pink and her eyes widen. "I can't imagine that."

I huff out an annoyed laugh. Thinking about it still pisses me off. "I was eighteen, and I knew her from school. Her dad was a producer and threw an enormous party. It was terrible and awkward, but because people got busted for other reasons, we were in the news for weeks. She ate up every minute of it while I just hid away."

"You're making a pretty good case not to move to LA."

"What about you?" I chance a glance up at her, but Gemma's gaze is fixed on the view.

"What about me?"

"What about your first time?"

"You don't need to know," she answers quickly.

"Oh, come on. I told you about mine. Hell, you can google my name and it still comes up. It's buried, but if you dig hard enough it's there."

"It looks like it might rain. We should head back." Gemma stands so quickly, it gives me whiplash.

"I don't see a single cloud in the sky."

She circles a finger around, looking nervous. "It's the mountains. The weather can change on a dime."

"You look like someone lit your ass on fire." I grab her arm to stop her, and she's looking everywhere but me.

It's almost as if she doesn't want me to know something.

"Wait, are you…"

I don't want to say the words. I don't want to be wrong.

Gemma turns to look at me this time. Something flares hot and bright in her eyes before disappearing.

"Shit. You are, aren't you?"

Taking a step back, Gemma explodes. "Yes, I'm a virgin. Are you happy?"

"Wait—"

"You men act like it's such a big deal." She interrupts me, acting like I'm not here. "It's not. My high school boyfriend was terrible and was only with me because he liked this girl who liked my brother who he dumped and then she spread horrible rumors about me because she was upset. So she convinced him to date me, but then he cheated on me with her to get back at me for what my brother did. And frankly, none of the men in town are all that appealing. And dating in Jackson, after going there for college, where the options are limited, makes it even harder. So after a certain point, I just kind of gave up. Happy?"

Her brown eyes are fierce as she stares me down. "That's a lot to unpack."

"I mean, have you met your species? Not that much, really."

I take a hesitant step toward her, treating her like a scared animal that might run off at a moment's notice.

"It sounds like your high school boyfriend was a dick, and I'm sorry they did that to you."

Gemma blows out a breath, like all the wind in her sails left. "He really was. He strung me along. We went to a party together, and that's when I found them together. It crushed me. It's what made dating so hard too. It was hard to trust people after that."

We're left staring at each other, neither one of us knowing what to say. The wind kicks up around us. It feels good after the hike.

Hell, it's calming me down after Gemma's revelation. It draws me to her even more. There's something about this woman that I can't pinpoint that I like. Something about her confession makes it easier to trust her.

Hell, ever since I arrived here, nothing about Gemma has been what I expected. There's no airs about her. What you see is exactly what you get. Probably why I *can* trust her.

And the number of people I trust can probably be counted on one hand.

I take a few steps closer to her. Up close, freckles dot Gemma's face. No doubt from spending so much time outdoors.

"I'm sorry I made you tell me all that."

"It's fine. Just not something I enjoy advertising. I feel like people think there's something wrong with you if you're not giving it up the first chance you get."

I laugh, brushing a few wayward strands of hair behind her ear. "I don't think there's anything wrong with that, Gemma."

Her head tilts toward my hand. "We really should get back. When it gets cool like this, it typically means rain will follow."

"You really don't have to keep lying about that." I smile down at her.

Her eyes reflect the sun. Almost like it's inside of her and fighting to get out.

"I'm not lying."

As if on cue, a few drops fall from the sky. Looking up, I see the sun is shining brightly over the ranch, but behind the mountains, dark clouds have moved in.

"Shit, you really weren't."

"Stick with me, Blake. I'll teach you a thing or two."

Her words settle into me as we pack up and race down the trail.

There's something I'd like to teach her.

If only I could think of a way to get her on board.

Chapter Eight

GEMMA

"You here alone tonight, Gem?" Nash, Peter's boyfriend, asks. When he's not busy planning his big music festival in town this summer, he helps out at the bar with Peter.

"Ivy should be here any minute."

"Can I get you something while you wait?"

"The Clara, please."

The Clara, the bar's best-selling drink. Named for Peter's high school girlfriend. They were each other's beards. Peter is now happily with his partner, Nash, and Clara moved to Jackson with her wife. She's treated like royalty anytime she comes to town.

"What brings you two out tonight?"

I shrug out of my jacket as The Tipsy Cocktail starts to fill up. "With her starting her new job, I haven't seen her a lot lately."

He sets a copper mug in front of me. "One Clara."

"Why is this so good?" I sip on the cocktail. Ginger explodes on my tongue, cutting the taste of the vodka. It's the perfect refreshing drink.

"It's a good thing your brother isn't here, otherwise he'd have a long-winded speech about how he makes the best drinks in town."

"I hear that enough at home. Thanks, Nash."

"You got it." He heads down the bar as a familiar brunette rushes inside.

"Hi! Hi! I know, I'm late. Sorry!" Ivy runs to where I'm sitting in a whirlwind of perfume.

"Ivy. You've been running late since I met you. Why would tonight be any different?" I laugh, sipping my drink.

"Blame Willow."

"You're really blaming my niece? That sweet girl?"

Ivy drops into the seat next to me. "Yes. She didn't want Daisy to be cold and had to get her a sweater. But she kept saying Daisy didn't like the ones she had. And when I told her Daisy is a dog and doesn't care, I got an entire speech about how she knows what she likes. It was a whole thing."

I laugh. "That sounds about right."

"Anyway, I was able to get her over to Gramps's without too much trouble."

"It's going well though?"

Ivy beams at me. "It is. She's a firecracker."

"She gets it from her dad, that's for sure."

Something flashes across Ivy's face, but it's gone before I can pick up on it.

"Hey, Ivy. You want anything to drink?" Peter comes up.

"Hey, Peter. I'll have whatever Gem is having."

He laughs. "You guys know that you can drink something other than the Clara, right?"

"It's your best drink." Ivy flashes him a bright smile.

"It is. But it also doesn't mean you can't order something else."

"I'm good."

Peter mixes her drink for her. "And Mason's been okay?"

"He's a peach."

"Our brother? A peach?" Peter interjects. "No one has ever described Mason that way."

"Maybe he's a better boss than you are," Ivy tells him.

"You realize I'm his boss, right?" Peter tells her. "And I'm making your drink."

He sets it in front of her.

"Mason's good to me. Don't worry."

"If you say so." Peter taps the bar in front of us. "Holler if you need a refill."

"Thanks, Peter."

Ivy's eyes slide over me. "You look great, by the way." When the two of us come out, I don't usually get so dressed up.

The silk black camisole I'm wearing shows off just enough cleavage without exposing too much, and the black jeans do wonders for my ass. I even put a little wing on my eyeliner.

Why do I look so good?

I hoped to see Blake before leaving the ranch. But I didn't.

I hate that I was so disappointed. He wasn't staked out at his usual spot in the lobby. I've become so accustomed to him being there, that it threw me when he wasn't.

"Thanks." I take a long pull on my drink.

"Trying to impress anyone?" Ivy waggles her brows at me.

"I wanted to look nice. Sue me."

"It's not because of that hot new guy lurking around the ranch?"

"Lurking? Really, Ivy?"

"Since Mrs. Phillips got wind of him being here, it's all anyone in town can talk about."

"He's nice."

"Nice?" Ivy rolls her eyes so hard, I'm afraid they'll fall out of her head. "Please. The weather today was nice. Can't you give me something better than that?"

I give her a coy smile. "What constitutes as better?"

Her eyes grow wide. "I think you know what better I mean."

I laugh. "We went hiking. I saw his abs."

"God, I must really need sex if I'm drooling over the thought of you seeing his abs."

"Ivy!" My face flushes.

"What? Don't tell me the thought hasn't crossed your mind."

My cheeks must pinken even more because Ivy points an accusatory finger in my direction. "Wait a minute! You have, haven't you?" she shrieks.

"No." I shush her and peer around. The bar has gotten crowded the later it's gotten. Maybe because it's one of the only places open past eight. "But it might have come up."

"How does the subject of your virginity just come up?" She throws up air quotes around her last words.

"We were getting to know one another."

"You told him?" Ivy barks out.

"It came up."

"I'd like something else of his to come up."

"Ivy!" I smack her arm. "That's crude."

"What?" She nurses her own drink. "I'm just saying what everyone else is thinking. I'd climb him like a tree, and I'm not even that into him."

"Is that what everyone's saying?" I look around the bar, as if every person here is interested in Blake.

"He's a hot commodity. It's not every day that we get someone that's as attractive as he is coming to town."

She's right. As much as I want to deny it, Blake is hot. Whenever he wiped the sweat from his brow on our hike, it exposed a gorgeous set of abs. And that crooked smile of his? I want to kiss it.

"It doesn't mean you need to spend all night ogling him."

Ivy rests her elbow on the bar and drops her chin in hand. "Is that because you want to ogle him?"

I down the rest of my own drink and signal for Nash.

"Need another?"

"Desperately."

"Hey!" Ivy smacks me on the arm this time. "I'm just trying to get you to see that you like him."

"Like whom?" Nash asks, mixing a drink with ease.

"The new guy." Ivy waggles her brows at Nash.

"Blake?" Nash turns his focus to me. "He's straight as a whistle, and I'll admit he's hot."

"You shouldn't say that," I tell him as he sets my drink in front of me.

"Why not? I have eyes. It's not like I'm going to go after him."

"Who are you not going after?" Peter comes up next to him.

"Blake Travers."

"Think he'd be up for a threesome?" Peter asks Nash.

Nash thumbs over his shoulder at me. "Considering Gemma here has the hots for him, I don't think we should."

"See? Even these two see it, and they can't see past one another."

It's true. Ever since Nash came back into my brother's

life, they've been so loved up, it's disgusting. Or would be disgusting if not for everything they went through.

"We're not that bad." Peter glares at us.

"That's not what Mason said last week." Ivy sips on her drink, a sly look on her face.

Based on the fact that both Peter and Nash's faces turn bright red, I don't want more details.

I shoo them away. "As wonderful as this conversation is, please go back to work."

"Thank God." They both leave us, walking a little too close together toward the office.

"They really are adorable."

I pluck the cherry out of my drink and pop it in my mouth. "I'm really happy for them."

It's then that someone across the bar catches my eye—someone I don't recognize.

"Ooh, what have we here?" Ivy asks, swiveling on her barstool.

"Please don't draw attention to us."

"If you don't plan on going after Blake, you could have a fun night with those guys."

"I don't know them."

Ivy slaps my arm. "Makes it even better. We know too much about all the guys around here."

Downfalls of a small town.

I sip my drink, casting another glance in their direction. "They are cute."

"They are. Why don't you go talk to them?"

I don't know why I'm hesitating. It's not like Blake is here to be the focus of my attention.

"You're overthinking it," Ivy tells me.

"Are you going to go over there with me? There's two of them, and it's not like you're seeing anyone."

Ivy picks up her drink and slams down the rest of it.
"Okay, fine. Let's go."
She stands, holding her hand out for me.
I guess we're doing this.

Chapter Nine

"Hey, the man of the hour!" A man with brown hair greets me as I find my spot at the bar.

"Nice to meet you…"

"Peter. Peter Winchester."

"One of Gemma's brothers."

He quirks a brow in my direction. "We've heard a lot about you."

"Oh, really?"

"Words gets around the Winchester family."

"Ah."

"Can I get you something to drink?" Peter asks.

"Whatever you recommend."

"How's your project going?" Peter is expertly mixing my drink behind the bar.

"You know about my project?"

Peter laughs. "Small town. And like I said, nothing stays secret in the Winchester family."

I'm more than flattered that Gemma's told her family about me.

"It's been going a lot better than I thought it would."

"Glad to hear our small town is inspiring you."

"Something like that."

I don't want to tell him that his sister is the one that's inspiring. I figured I'd be blocked and it would be a slog to get any words out. The way she talks about this place has made the words flow. Instead of breaking that concentration to head to my spot in the lobby, I stayed in my cabin tonight.

Turns out, all I needed was Gemma for the words to flow.

When I went to find Gemma to see if she wanted to grab a drink, she wasn't around. A drink in town was a close second.

"Here you go."

Grabbing the copper mug, I sip the drink. "Damn, that's good."

"Thanks. Created it myself."

"You own the place?" Gemma never mentioned her brother owned the place.

"Even make the vodka."

"Damn." I take another long pull on the drink. "How'd you get into that business?"

Peter shrugs a shoulder. "How'd you get into the Hollywood business?"

"Family business you could say. Brewing vodka a family business?"

Peter laughs at me. "You don't brew vodka."

"Fine, then. Whatever you do with vodka."

"Distill. Seemed like an interesting enough thing to do. I was never really interested in running the ranch, so Gramps helped me with this."

"He sounds like a good guy."

Peter pours himself a glass of water. "You haven't met him yet?"

I shake my head. "I haven't."

"He's always around the ranch. Loves popping in and checking on Gemma."

"Why's that?" I ask.

"She's the baby of the family. We joke she's the favorite, but those two have always had a special relationship."

"Do I need to be worried about him?"

Peter rests his elbows on the bar, glugging down his water. "I don't know, do you?"

Considering the thoughts I've had about his granddaughter? Yeah, I feel like I should be worried. I came here fully expecting to be hunkered away for a few weeks while writing my script.

"I don't think so."

Peter smiles back at me. "No, you should be worried about Mason."

"Mason? Your older brother, Mason?"

If possible, his smile gets even bigger. "I take it you haven't met him."

"Let me clear this up for you. You're the only sibling I've met of Gemma's."

"Oh man. You've got your work cut out for you."

"It's not like we're dating."

Although, based on how he's grilling me, you'd think we are. Not that I'm opposed to the idea. Even if I really don't have the time while I'm here.

"Okay." Peter shrugs his shoulder.

"I'm serious."

"Whatever you say."

"I'm just in town for a few weeks. Nothing will happen."

And maybe if I tell myself that enough, I might start to

believe it. I haven't been able to get Gemma out of my head since crashing into her.

"Oh, fuck me." Peter's voice grabs my attention. I follow his line of sight. Two women are standing on the outskirts of what appears to be a makeshift dance floor as two guys look like they're about ready to throw punches.

And one of those women?

Gemma.

What the fuck?

Peter hops over the bar and I follow him over to where a crowd is growing.

"Everything okay over here?"

"We were just leaving." The guy gives me a cocky smirk. What an ass.

One of the guys goes to grab Gemma's friend, but she shrugs him off. "And we said we weren't leaving with you."

"So you'll dance with us but not go home with us?"

"Dancing doesn't lead to sex. Unless you're from that town from Footloose." Her friend rolls her eyes.

Hearing the way these two are talking about Gemma and her friend has my blood boiling. Fucking assholes.

One of the guys elbows his friend. "C'mon, man, they're not worth it."

"Maybe you two should treat them with a little more respect." I take a step closer. I'm fuming. Guys like these dicks are rampant in LA. It's one of the reasons I hate going out to the fancy bars. The small pubs near my place in Malibu are way more chill. Kind of like this place.

"Blake, don't worry about them." Gemma grabs my arm, pulling me back.

"You can't let them get away with this shit."

"We're fine." Gemma moves her hands to my chest, pushing me back. It's what finally gets my attention. "Ivy and I are fine. We know how to handle ourselves."

I blow out a breath. "You sure?"

I finally have a minute to take her in. She looks fine.

Peter and Nash escort the two assholes out of the bar.

"What the fuck is going on here?" A new booming voice enters the room.

"Mason. What are you doing here?" Ivy sounds surprised he's here. I take in the hulking, angry beast that fills the door. Holy shit. This is Gemma's other brother? He looks like he could squash me like a bug.

"Got a text that a fight was about to break out. I was down the street, so figured I'd stop in."

"Mason, we've got it taken care of," Peter tells him. "Just a couple of drunk idiots wanting to take them home."

"What the hell do you two think you're doing?" Mason turns his angry eyes on Gemma.

"Mason, we're twenty-three. We're allowed to dance with guys if we want to."

Now that the two guys are gone, everyone is starting to go back to their drinks.

"Not if you're going to start fights."

"Would you relax, Mason?" Ivy tells him. "God, why are you being like this?"

It wouldn't surprise me to see steam shooting out of his eyes as he locks eyes with Ivy. The two of them look like they're ready to scream at each other.

"I wouldn't have to if you didn't insist on coming out tonight."

"Oh, fuck off, Mason! We weren't doing anything wrong!"

"Umm, are these two going to be okay?" I whisper to Gemma.

Peter, Nash, Gemma, and now the people around us, are staring at these two fighting.

"Why is Mason so worked up?" Peter asked.

"This is even better than reality TV." Nash's eyes are bouncing between the two of them.

Gemma leans ever so slightly into me.

"You okay?" I ask, wrapping an arm around her shoulders. The minute my fingers touch her exposed shoulder, goose bumps break out over her skin.

"Ready to get out of here."

"Mason," I call out, interrupting the two fuming people in front of us. "I'm taking Gemma home. Will you make sure Ivy gets home?"

His nods, giving me an approving look.

Huh. Maybe he's not so hard to win over.

"Thanks." Mason turns a hard eye on Peter. "Can you maybe not let them drink so much next time?"

"Hey. They're not drunk. You guys just got shitty that they were dancing with other people. Don't blame me."

Mason growls again.

"Let's go," I murmur to Gemma.

"Wait. I need my coat."

Gemma runs over to where she was sitting, waves goodbye at Peter and Nash, and makes her way back over to me.

I want to reach out to her. Take her hand in mine. Devour her lips that look fucking perfect right now.

But I can't. She's not mine to take.

Opening the door, I help Gemma into the front seat and run around the car.

There's a bite to the air still. Even though spring is right around the corner, winter is still hanging on.

We're both quiet as I point the car back toward the ranch. It's not an uncomfortable silence.

"I didn't see you tonight." Gemma breaks the silence.

"You're seeing me right now."

"I meant at the ranch. You weren't in your usual spot."

"You noticed?"

The roads are dark as we leave town. This is not something I'm used to. In LA, there are lights everywhere. No matter what time of day it is, there's always someone out.

This is something I could get used to.

"I've gotten used to seeing you at your desk."

"It's my desk now?"

"Yes." Out of the corner of my eye, I see Gemma shift in her seat to fully face me. "Out of all the years I've been working here, you're the only person I've seen use it."

"Maybe no one else found it inspiring."

"And you have?"

"I have."

I turn onto the ranch's property. It's a quick drive when we're the only people on the road.

"Where do you usually find inspiration?" Gemma asks.

"What's with all the questions?"

"Curious is all."

The ranch comes into view up ahead.

"Turn right here. It'll take you back to my cabin."

I follow Gemma's instructions as she points me to a small cabin tucked into the woods.

"Thanks for the ride, Blake."

"Let me walk you to your door."

"I'll be okay." Gemma unlocks her seatbelt and gets out of the car. I do the same, running around to meet her.

"What if you get attacked by a bear?"

Gemma leans back against the car, crossing her arms. "And you know the first thing about defending us from a bear?"

"Well, not exactly."

"Guess someone didn't read the guidebook in their cabin."

I follow Gemma up to her front porch like a lost little puppy.

"You got me. But hey, looks like we're safe from bears."

I flash a smile at Gemma. Under the glow of her porch light, she is fucking stunning. It's a halo around her. Her brown hair shimmers and those eyes of hers are soft as they take me in.

Kiss her.

The feeling overwhelms me, like if I don't kiss her, I might die.

Gemma has other ideas though. Keys in hand, she goes to unlock her front door, but drops the keys.

"Shit."

"Here, let me."

It'll give my brain a minute to come back to center.

Gemma leans against the door as I fiddle with the key. Her coat opens to the silky top she's wearing. It dips low. The gold compass necklace she wears sits at the top of her cleavage. One that I wouldn't mind running my tongue over.

Fuck. I don't think she knows how sexy she really is.

"Having trouble?" Gemma asks.

"It's a door. I can manage."

If only Gemma wasn't standing so close to me.

Finally getting the key in, I unlock the door and push it open for Gemma.

"Sorry for all the trouble tonight, Blake." Gemma shrugs out of her coat, flinging it over the back of the couch. She leans against it.

"I'm glad you're okay."

Gemma shrugs. "They were harmless. But I am glad you were there."

"Why's that?" I take a step closer to her.

"I missed seeing you."

"You did?"

Gemma's fiddling with the necklace adorning her chest. She nods.

"Why?"

"Because"—it's like she's gauging how much she wants to tell me—"because I like you, Blake."

The urge is back.

"How much have you had to drink, Gemma?"

"What? Why?"

"Because I want to kiss you, but if you've had too much to drink, I'm not going to do it."

Her eyes widen. They're darker tonight. "I had one drink. Nash tends to water them down a little too much."

I close the distance between us. One hand goes to her neck, the other to her hip. Warm skin meets mine. Gemma is just as soft as I imagined her to be. Gemma's hands fist in my shirt.

"Can I kiss you, Gemma?"

Her tongue darts out to lick her lips. "Yes."

I want nothing more than to ravage her lips, but I don't. My thumb swipes across her lips. She tilts her head up.

Gemma wants this as much as I do.

Touching my forehead to hers, our hot breaths mingle. I catch the faintest wisp of vodka and cherries on her lips.

I drop my hand to her jaw, brushing my fingertips along the tender skin there. Her breath stutters. The pulse in her neck is throbbing.

Anticipation is killing her as much as it's killing me.

It's then that I finally close the distance between the two of us.

And holy fuck. It's the softest of kisses, but it has my blood boiling. I want to feast on her lips. Make up for every minute I haven't spent kissing her.

I've never felt anything like it.

Gemma must feel it too because she gasps. I take the opportunity to tangle my tongue with hers.

I swallow her gasps and moans. She pulls me even closer to her, the tips of her fingers squeezing me tight.

A kiss shouldn't be making me this hard, but it is.

All I want to do is take her into her bedroom and have my way with her, but that's not what this is about. Not what her first time should be. Gemma deserves more than that.

With great reluctance, I pull back. Her plump lips are wet as Gemma eyes me.

"Wow."

"Damn right, wow."

"Why'd you stop?" She fights a yawn.

I drop one more kiss to her lips. Spotting her bedroom, I lead her back that way.

"Because you deserve more than a hurried fuck for your first time."

Gemma's tired so I don't hesitate as I pull back the comforter.

"Why couldn't you have been my high school boyfriend?"

"What?" What in the world is she talking about?

Sleep is clearly overcoming her as she sinks under her duvet.

"Why couldn't you have been the one to take my V-card in high school?"

And then she's out.

Holy shit.

Now there's about a million different thoughts racing through my head as I tuck Gemma into bed.

But none more so than that kiss. Those whispered words.

Because now that she mentioned her V-card, it's all I can think about.

Sex with Gemma.

Something tells me that kiss was just the start of things between us.

And I can't wait to see where they go.

Chapter Ten

GEMMA

"Rise and shine, Gemma." A knock on my front door and Blake's voice pull me from sleep, and I stumble to open the door for him.

"It's too early," I mutter as I go straight back to bed and pull the covers over my head.

"It's almost ten."

I peek one eye open and pull the covers back down. The delicious scent of coffee fills my nose. "I hope one of those is for me."

He hands me the mug. "Feeling okay?"

"Why wouldn't I be?"

Sitting up, I pull the blankets around me.

"You and Ivy had quite the night."

"It's not usually like that."

"What is a usual Saturday night like for you?" Blake takes a seat on the edge of my bed.

"Either wine here at the ranch, or a drink at the bar. Dancing and getting into fights is not usually on the agenda."

"Good to know that's not the norm."

"Oh, crap." I reach over to the nightstand, grabbing my phone. I'm still in my clothes from last night. "Ivy didn't text me back last night."

There's a text waiting from her.

IVY

I'm fine. You okay?

Good. I'm fine too

"SORRY." I turn my attention back to the man sitting by me.

"Don't be. It was probably the most exciting night I've had since coming here."

"Sorry Dixon isn't keeping you entertained." I fight the eye roll, sipping from the steaming mug of coffee.

"Don't put words into my mouth, Gemma." Blake eyes me, drinking from his own mug. "Dixon is keeping me plenty entertained."

"So last night was good then?"

"Last night was very good. Especially the ending."

My cheeks heat at the thought of that kiss. I thought I knew what a good kiss was. Apparently not. Turns out, I've been neglected if Blake's kiss is any indication of how good it can be.

"Good."

"Much better than good, Gemma. Do I need to remind you how good?" Blake takes the mug out of my hand, placing it on the nightstand.

His presence is overwhelming in my small bedroom. He leans over, grabbing my chin with those fingers. Fingers that I'm pretty sure I dreamt about last night.

Hot breath ghosts over my lips. It's the hint of a tease. A hint of what's to come. A whimper escapes my lips before Blake's mouth makes the softest contact with mine.

I'm arching into him, needing and wanting more from him. Last night wasn't enough.

His tongue slides across the seam of my lips, and I grant him entry. My hands fist in his shirt, pulling him tighter.

Heat is gathering in my core. I haven't felt this way in a long time.

One of the downsides of growing up in a small town is you know everyone. Every sordid detail of every guy's past. Who they dated. Whose heart they broke.

Now that Blake's here, he's all I can think about, and I don't have to worry about any of those things with him.

He pulls back.

"I have a proposition for you."

"Oh, yeah? I hope it involves more of that."

I want Blake to stop talking and start kissing me again.

He smiles against my lips. "If you agree, then there will definitely be more of that."

"Go on."

"I think you and I could enter into a mutually benefi-cial relationship."

"Blake, get to the point."

"I need help figuring out the finer points of western life, and you, based on your comments last night, could use some help navigating sex."

"What?" I shove Blake back, flying out of bed. "You can't bring this up before I've even had coffee!"

My voice sounds shrieky. I don't think anyone has ever propositioned me for sex before.

No, I know so.

"You're the one who brought it up last night."

"Me? No, I didn't." I really need to get my voice under control. I'm approaching a volume only dogs can hear.

"Would you like me to remind you?"

"Stop saying it like that."

"Like what?" Blake gives me a cunning grin. He knows exactly what he's doing.

And I hate that I'm letting him get to me.

"Like you know what I look like naked." I point a finger at him. "Because you don't."

"But I could."

That shuts me up.

I can't help but let my eyes rake over him. He's wearing the same thing from last night. I guess neither of us bothered to change.

My eyes shoot back up to meet his. That same smile is staring back at me.

"But…how? Why? Just…why?"

I'm stunned speechless. Something that seems to happen around this guy.

"Do you need a minute?"

"What I need is more details."

"Do you want to go into the living room and talk about it?"

It's then I notice the unmade bed between us. "Yes."

I stalk out of the room, needing some space from the man who has been driving me crazy since I first ran into him.

"Is this better?"

Blake is standing on the opposite end of the couch from me.

I nod.

"Good. What questions do you have?"

"What questions don't I have?" I mutter to myself.

"It's easier to ask the questions, Gem."

Gem.

I like the sound of my nickname rolling off his tongue.

"Why?"

"Why?" he parrots back.

"You told me to ask questions. This is me asking you the questions, Blake."

He smirks at my response.

"I need help."

"What do you need help with?"

"My show."

"What's wrong with it?"

He shakes his head. "Nothing. There's nothing to be wrong because I'm not really getting anywhere with it. I got a little done this morning, but if I want to make this story work, I need help."

"With family drama?"

Blake huffs out a tiny laugh.

"With this western stuff. I'd love to set it here."

It dawns on me now. "And you'd have no idea how to make that work since you've only ever lived in Paris and LA."

"Exactly. And I don't want to just take from you."

"Except you kind of do." I laugh.

Blake snorts, rubbing his hand over his jaw. "I wouldn't phrase it like that."

"How would you phrase it then?" I cross my arms over my chest.

He takes a minute. "Not like that."

"So I teach you how to ride a horse and you teach me how to ride you?"

"Jesus, Gemma." He snorts out a laugh. "Definitely not like that."

"But kind of like that."

"Think about it. I could make it really good for you."

That, I do not doubt. Based off that kiss alone, it would be mind-blowing.

"I'm not some blushing daisy," I blurt out. "You don't need to handle me with kid gloves."

"I never said you were."

"And it's not like I have no experience."

"No?" Blake sips his coffee, casual as ever.

"There was some hand action below the belt. And I am well-acquainted with my vibrator."

"Fuck."

I don't miss the heated look in Blake's eyes. It's good to know that I'm not the only one invested in this thing. Whatever this thing might be.

"Look. I don't want this to be a pity kind of thing." I voice the worry that prickles at the edge of my thoughts.

"You think this is a pity thing?"

I shrug a shoulder.

Blake sets down his coffee cup and moves around the couch. He looms large over me.

He crushes his lips to mine, stealing my breath.

And any fight I might have.

This kiss is every bit as good as it was last night.

Maybe even better because I thought I was imagining it last night.

Blake controls the kiss. Nipping and sucking on my bottom lip. It has my toes curling in the plush carpet.

I never want it to end.

But it does.

"Make no mistake. I want you, Gemma. Not out of pity. Not out of a need to take your virginity." Blake trails a single finger down my jaw. My neck. Over the curve of my shoulder. "If you can't tell how much I want you, then I might need to kiss you again."

"You might need to kiss me again, then."

He smiles before taking one more kiss.

"Think about it, Gemma."

I nod.

"Say it."

"I'll think about it."

"Good girl."

Two words.

Good girl.

They have butterflies swarming in my stomach. I want to hear them again. I want to hear them as Blake thrusts inside of me.

It hits me out of nowhere. I haven't made much effort in dating over the last few years. I didn't really see the point when I know everyone in Dixon. No one was really worth making an effort for.

Now, a few weeks surrounded by this man, and I'm ready to give him everything.

"Don't answer me yet."

"Why not?"

"I want you to think about it. Really think about it. It's a big decision."

Blake's right. It is.

It's also one that I'm fairly certain I want to say yes to.

"I have to get going, Gemma. But I promise you, I'll make it good for you."

Bending over, Blake stuffs his feet into his shoes. My eyes don't stray from how good his ass looks in those jeans.

Ogling Blake is my new favorite thing. And all too soon, he's almost out the door.

"I'll see you around the ranch."

"I hope you'll be seeing a lot more of me."

With a wink, he's out the door.

I will definitely be seeing all that man has to offer.

Gemma Winchester won't be a virgin much longer.

Chapter Eleven

BLAKE

Holy shit.

This is good. This is really good.

It's like a switch was flipped.

For the first time in what feels like months, words are coming easily to me. There's no niggling fear of self-doubt sitting in the back of my mind. This is something I'm proud of. Something I'm actually excited to send to Clint.

The buzzing of my phone cuts through my work.

Speak of the devil.

I swipe to answer. "Hey Clint."

"Blake. How's it going in…where are you again?"

"Idaho."

"Idaho. I don't know where that is."

Typical Clint. If it's not a major metropolis, he has no interest. Even though I've told him every single time he's called.

"What's going on?"

"How's the writing going?"

"You mean the writing you forced upon me?" I save the document and close my laptop.

One can never be too careful with saving your work.

"Don't be so dramatic."

I lean back onto the couch, grabbing my wine and taking a long sip. Damn, that's good.

I didn't have the first clue what the food would be like here, but every meal is better than the last.

"It's going."

"Do you have something I can look at?"

"Not yet."

"Listen, Blake. You know I love you like a son, but I need more than that. You're like a dried-up ocean these last few months."

"Ouch."

"I say it with love." Even over the phone, I can picture that placating look he gives me.

"I'm hoping to have something to you in the next few weeks. I'm writing."

"And it's good?"

"Jesus. Give me a little more credit." I scrub a frustrated hand down my face. This is always part of the problem with Hollywood. You can't just write something.

It has to be good.

I don't want to tell Clint what I have right now—almost as if showing him might jinx the flow of ideas.

There's a soft knock at the door.

"Clint, I have to go."

"Got a hot date?"

Glancing through the peephole, that's exactly what I'm hoping to have. "Something like that."

I don't wait to hear his response before ending the call. Gemma's smile greets me as I swing open the door.

"Gemma. What are you doing here?" I sweep my arm out, welcoming her in.

"Sorry to bother you."

"It's no bother." I walk back into the living room and grab my wine, eyeing her carefully.

I shouldn't be so taken in by Gemma. My time here is limited.

"I was told that the kitchen forgot your wine and thought I'd bring it over."

"You mean this wine?" I swirl the glass I'm holding.

Her cheeks turn a fiery red. I love how much she blushes around me. It tells me she likes me.

"Bad information from the kitchen, I guess."

Walking over to her, I grab the bottle from her hand. "Care to split it with me?"

"Sure."

Gemma follows me into the kitchen. I grab fresh glasses for both of us. Popping it open, I pour us each a glass.

"Sorry you had to come all the way out here."

"No trouble." She sips her wine, a demure look on her face.

It's nothing like the look on her face the other night. The one after our kiss. The kiss—and proposition—that I can't seem to get out of my head.

"How's your writing going?"

"Did you really come over here to talk about that?"

Gemma shakes her head.

"Then what'd you come over here for?"

Setting down her wine, Gemma takes a step closer to me. "I think you know why."

I sip my own glass of wine. "Want to hear more about my proposition?"

I lean back against the counter, crossing my bare feet.

"Something like that."

"What do you want to talk about?"

"Why do you want to do this?"

"I like you, Gemma." My words are blunt.

"And that's enough for you?"

"What were the exact words you said?"

Gemma smiles at me, tucking a stray strand of hair behind her ear. "Something along the lines of how men suck."

"Oh, no." I set down my glass, taking a few steps toward her. "You said you've met my sex, is it any surprise I haven't given it up?"

"Okay, that." She sips on her wine.

"And I think I can say I'm different than most guys."

"Oh, yeah? How?"

There's that fierce fighting side of Gemma that I'm growing accustomed to. She's not like the women I'm used to in LA. The women I'm used to couldn't care less about most things. Likes, comments…those things interest them.

Not Gemma.

Gemma's all fresh air and mountains.

Horses and hiking.

Mucking out stalls one minute and then out at the bars the next.

"I'm not some two-bit chump for starters."

"Okay."

"I'd treat you right."

"Okay." Gemma's fighting a smile.

"I can make it good for you, Gemma."

"Convince me."

"What?" The woman walking toward me has shocked me speechless. "You want me to convince you to have sex with me?"

Her fingers walk up my chest, hardening my dick in my pants.

"You say you can make it good?"

"Yes."

One word. All confidence. I know I can rock her world.

"Then convince me."

I look around at my small cabin. "Right now?"

"If you don't think you can…"

She spins on her heel and walks toward the door. I don't let her open it, setting my hand by her head.

"You want me to prove it to you?" My mouth is right by her ear. I can feel her shudder.

"Mm-hmm."

Sweeping her hair back, I expose her neck. Her vein pulses. Throbs.

"Let me show you." I drop my lips onto her neck, resting there. Not doing what I really want to be doing.

"Then show me."

"Come with me." I link my hand with hers, leading her into my room. Her eyes are wide.

Pulling her into the room behind me, I shut the door and spin her so her back is to it.

Emotions are swimming in her eyes. I love that Gemma wears her heart on her sleeve.

Gemma loops her fingers through my belt loops and pulls me closer to her. "Are you going to kiss me?"

"Do you want me to kiss you?"

"I wouldn't be asking you if I didn't."

"Here?" I kiss the edge of her jaw.

She groans. "No."

"What about here?" I kiss on that damn vein that is driving me crazy.

"Mmm."

"You like that?"

I kiss her there again, sucking on the tender skin there. Nibbling.

"Yes."

I continue doing it, moving to the other side. Taking

slow steps, I walk us back to the bed. Her knees hit the mattress and she collapses back.

The connection between us is broken—only for a moment—but it's too long. I want to keep my lips on her.

I settle over her, one of her legs hiking up over my hips.

"What have you done before?"

"What?" Her voice is breathless as she squirms under me.

"You said you have some experience."

I keep kissing her. She keeps arching into my touch. Needing more. Wanting more.

"Tell me, Gemma. Tell me what you want me to do to you tonight."

Small but sure fingers wrap around mine and drag them lower and lower. Brushing over the soft fabric that hides her pussy from me.

"Here. I want you to touch me here."

Fuck. I drag my fingers back up, pushing her shirt up.

Stretching my body next to hers, I ghost my fingers over the waistband of her pants, pushing below them. I push past the edge of her underwear.

Keep going lower.

And lower.

The heat and soft curls of her pussy meet my fingers. The feel of her has my dick hardening in my pants. I slip one finger between her folds. She's already wet.

"Fuck, Gemma."

Her hand grabs me, pushing me farther. She's needy.

And I fucking love it.

I dip one finger inside. She's tight, but takes me without too much trouble.

There's no rush. My palm grinds down on her clit as I work my finger in and out of her, then add another.

Gemma is a squirming mess beneath me. Her nails are digging into my forearm.

I know she's close. Instead of going faster, I slow down, drawing out her pleasure as best I can. Every squeeze of her pussy on my fingers has me imagining it is my cock and wanting to feel how tight she is as I sink into her.

I growl and nip at the tender skin of Gemma's jaw.

If this woman doesn't say yes after this, I might have to turn tail and run.

Because now that I mentioned it, it's all I fucking want.

"Yes! Yes! Yes!" Gemma starts chanting as she comes on my fingers. I work her through it, slowly moving in and out of her.

"Oh my God. So good."

My smile is smug as Gemma turns her eyes on me. She's focused on me as I pull my fingers out of her. As I take them in my mouth. Suck off her release.

Her eyes are greedy as she watches.

It's not like we had sex or anything, but it might be one of the hottest things I've ever witnessed. Watching Gemma come undone at my hand?

Sexy as fuck.

"Do you want me to take care of you?" Gemma's hands trail over the hard planes of my chest, drifting lower to the bulge in my jeans.

"No."

"What do you mean no?"

I pull her hand off me. I don't need to blow in my pants. Nothing would be more uncomfortable than that.

"I mean no. I can take care of myself. Today is about you. Proving to you that I'll take care of you."

"I think you might need to prove that point again." A relaxed smile flirts on her lips.

"You need more?"

"Need. Want. More."

Her words are broken.

"I take it that means you're accepting my proposal?"

"Your terms are agreeable."

"Agreeable?"

She nods, still basking in pleasure in bed.

In *my* bed.

"I'm glad you find them agreeable. Because there will be plenty more of this."

"Good. Because I want more. I want it all."

"You'll get it all."

And I can't fucking wait.

Chapter Twelve

GEMMA

"Gem, would you c'mere for a minute?" Gramps calls from the office behind the front desk.

"What's going on?" I drop into the chair across from his desk.

"Do you know anything about these orders for new mattresses for the guest cabins?"

I take the invoice he hands to me. "No. Why would I know anything about that?"

"It was back before Jenny left."

"Gramps, I don't know why she did it. She didn't clue me in to her inner workings as manager."

He sighs, leaning back in his chair. "You worked closely with her, so I thought you might know why."

It's the perfect opportunity to talk to him again about why he doesn't need to be handling this. "You know I could take this off your plate…"

"It's easier to handle myself."

When our manager left earlier this winter, it was the perfect chance for me to finally get what I've been working for. Except that Logan's injury derailed it.

Not that I'm blaming him. I wouldn't wish what happened to Logan on anyone. But instead of letting me take the reins, Gramps stepped back into the position. Said he didn't want to have to worry about the ranch while worrying about Logan too.

"But I know how to do this stuff."

Gramps leans back in his chair, his mustache twitching. "I need you to keep doing what you're doing. I rely on you to keep this place running."

"But—"

Gramps cuts me off. "Listen, they're talking about a severe storm blowing through tonight. Will you check with the staff that everyone has what they need so no one has to go out in it? Just in case."

I blow out a frustrated breath. He trusts me enough to do everything that he should be doing, but I'm still just punching the clock. Before, Gramps didn't want to promote me because he didn't want to step on the manager's toes. Now with her gone, it's just another excuse.

I hate how frustrating it is to get him to take me seriously. Why wouldn't he want a Winchester running the family ranch?

"I'll make sure everyone is taken care of."

"I appreciate it."

He goes back to work as I head back out to my desk, making calls and getting everyone squared away.

It's easy work. Something I'm used to, as we do this during the winter.

Maybe one day I won't be the one making the calls, but instead instructing others on how to do it.

The wind is picking up outside as the main door swings open.

"Aunt Gemma!"

Willow's face is happy as she races over to me.

"There's my favorite girl!"

She leaps into my open arms.

"I'm your only girl."

"Doesn't mean you aren't my favorite."

I turn my attention to my brother. He seems grumpier than usual.

"I really appreciate you taking her. Peter needs help closing down the bar."

"What kind of help?" I ask, setting Willow down. She goes over to the desk, setting down her backpack and taking out her homework folder.

"The kind that requires me to get over there now." His tone is short.

"Where's Ivy?"

"I don't know. It shouldn't take more than hour."

"It's fine. Just get back here before the storm hits."

"Thanks." He faces Willow. "Bye, Pipsqueak."

"Bye, Daddy!"

He turns without another word, his pissiness evident.

Willow's already hard at work on what looks to be math homework while I finish up the rest of my calls.

"Is the storm going to be bad, Aunt Gemma?"

"What makes you ask that?"

If it's anything like the weatherman is saying, we're in for a doozy. But I don't want to scare her.

"You're telling people not to come into work if it's too bad."

Damn. Willow is too smart for her own good.

"Better to be safe than sorry."

"I don't like storms," she tells me, dropping her pencil on her paper.

"You know what I used to do during storms when I was your age?"

She shakes her head.

"I used to sneak into your dad's room and sleep on his floor because I was scared."

Dark clouds are now rolling in. They're calling it the storm of the year—and it's not even summer yet. Thankfully the ranch isn't at capacity so it's not as bad as it could be.

"Do you think I can do that if I get scared?" she asks.

"Who's scared in here?"

Blake's smooth voice startles me.

"Me apparently," I mutter to myself.

"I don't like storms," Willow tells him matter-of-factly.

"What makes you happy?" He leans down onto the desk, getting down on Willow's level.

"Why?"

"If you're scared, think of what makes you happy." Blake turns those green eyes on me and winks.

Every inch of my body warms. I wish it didn't, that I could deny myself of him. But the more I'm around him, the more I want to be around him. And after the last time we were alone together?

It's all I can think about.

"Rainbows and Daddy and Daisy and my friends at school. And Aunt Gemma and Layla. And Uncle Peter and Logan. And football." Willow ticks everything off on her fingers one by one.

"Wow. That's a lot of happy things. If you think of them during the storm, you won't be scared."

She screws her tiny nose up in thought. "I don't know."

"Try it. I guarantee it'll work." Blake's confidence could win over anyone, yet Willow doesn't look impressed.

"If it doesn't, you have to help me write my story for school next week."

"Done." Blake holds out his hand for her to shake.

"But you can't make it an awful story." Willow points her finger at him. "Your sundae skills need work."

"Everyone's a critic. I promise, I don't write awful stories." He laughs.

"Do they have unicorns?"

"Well, no."

Willow shakes her head. "Then I don't know how good they are."

"Wow." Blake shifts his attention to me. "Guess I have my work cut out for me."

"She's not one to go easy on you."

The office door creaks open. "You're staying with me tonight, Pipsqueak." Gramps's deep voice echoes in the quiet lobby.

"Won't Daddy be scared?" Willow runs up to him and wraps her arms around his waist.

"He said someone had to stay with me, so I don't get scared."

Her eyes widen. "You get scared too?"

"Not if I have you." He lifts her into his arms. "How about we pitch a tent in the living room and pop some popcorn, hmm?"

"Yes!" She wraps her arms around him as they wander out of the lobby. "Bye, Aunt Gemma! Bye, Blake! Think happy thoughts!"

"Bye, sweetheart!" I shout after them. "You're great with her."

"She's a sweet kid. Just like her aunt."

I roll my eyes. "Laying it on pretty thick there, Blake."

Blake walks around the front desk, stopping in front of me. His scruff is thicker today.

I want to feel it on the inside of my thighs.

"Not if it's the truth."

I turn to leave, but he grabs me.

"Have you given any more thought to my offer?"

"If I had more than a minute of free time this week…"

The lie slips easily off my tongue. It's not like I haven't been busy this week. With one of the other girls calling in sick, and now prepping everything for the storm, it's been a chaotic few days.

The truth? It's all I've been thinking about. What it would be like to be with Blake. To give him that piece of me. Every time I'm around him, my need for him grows that much more.

"Pity." Blake licks his lips. I track the movement with greedy eyes. "Maybe you can spend tomorrow thinking about it."

One kiss from him and I'm hooked. The feel of his fingers inside of me and I want more. I know what I want to tell him. That my answer is an easy yes.

Only it's so much more than a simple yes.

The first raindrops pelt the tall windows. Even in the last few minutes, it's grown darker outside. "You should head back to your cabin. I don't want you getting caught out in the storm."

"Will you be okay, Gemma?"

My breath catches in my throat at his words. His dark eyes are laced with a hidden meaning.

I clear my throat, trying to find the words. "I'll be fine."

Blake brushes a piece of hair off my shoulder, his touch lingering. It sends goose bumps exploding across my skin.

His lips dip closer, ghosting the shell of my ear. "You know where to find me if you need anything."

I watch as he heads out the back door. The wind whips his hair around. It takes everything I have not to run after him.

I don't want to be that desperate girl, though, giving it up to the first guy who looks at me.

Except if it's anything like what we did the other night, it's going to be mind-blowing. So good, it'll rock my world and no one will ever compare to it.

Maybe that's why I'm holding out. But the longer Blake is here, the less willpower I have.

Who knew I'd be such a sucker for a city boy with green eyes?

Chapter Thirteen

GEMMA

"Holy shit."

The clap of thunder has me burrowing farther under the blankets on my couch. It's pitch black outside. Lightning cracks through the sky, illuminating everything.

The power went out an hour ago, but thankfully the generator kicked in immediately. I'd be in the fetal position if I had no power. Thankfully I have a bottle of wine I could open to try and settle my nerves.

I really hate thunderstorms.

Hail has been on and off all night. The rain pelts against the windows as a loud knock cuts through the sound of the wind.

"Oh my God!" It feels like my heart leapt out of my chest. I have no idea who would be out in this weather.

"Gemma! Open up!" The pounding starts again, but this time, my heart stays in my chest.

Wrapping the blanket around me, I run to the door. Blake fills the doorframe.

"What in the hell are you doing here?"

"The power went out." He shakes his hood out, spraying water everywhere.

"What? You have a generator."

He wipes the rain from his eyes. Even with a coat, he's sopping wet.

"Can we have this conversation inside?"

"Oh, sorry."

I grab his arm and tug him inside as another boom of thunder rattles the house.

I don't think. I lunge at him. Wrapping my arms around him, I hold on tight.

"Shit, you're shaking like a leaf." Blake squeezes his arms around me.

I nod against his chest. "I hate storms. I don't know why you chanced it and left your cabin."

Blake steps back, shrugging out of his jacket. "I didn't want to be without power for however long the storm lasts."

"I'll have someone look at it once this clears up." I wrap the blanket back around me and shuffle into the living room.

My eyes track Blake as he toes out of his shoes and pulls a sweatshirt over his head. It nearly takes his T-shirt off. It exposes a delicious set of abs and a trail of hair that disappears below his waistband.

"You okay over there?" he asks, following behind me.

"Yeah, I'm fine." My voice is squeaky.

"Because your face is red."

"No, it's not." I pat my cheeks, knowing full well that it's a lie.

"Whatever you say, Gemma."

"Can I get you a drink?" I change the subject.

"Sure." He stuffs his hands in his pockets. "What are you having?"

"Red wine." I head into the kitchen and grab a glass and the bottle.

"Sounds good to me." I pour him a glass and hand it to him. His fingers linger over mine. It's only for a second, but it's enough to set my blood pulsing through me.

I don't know what it is about this man that gets me going.

We're night and day.

Black and white.

City boy and country girl.

Experienced and, well, virgin.

We shouldn't mix, but we do.

"To waiting out the storm together." Blake holds his glass out, and I pick mine up to toast him.

"Did you get any writing done?"

"Some."

"That's good, right?"

"Very good. More than any writing I've gotten done in the last few months."

I shake my head. "What's inspiring you?"

His eyes sparkle. "Dixon. The ranch." He sits on the small loveseat that's facing the crackling fire. "You."

"Really?" I drop down next to him.

"Of course. The way you talk about this place? It'd be hard not to be inspired by that."

"That's nice of you," I tell him, tucking a piece of hair behind my ear.

Blake sips on his wine. "It might very well be the thing that saves my career."

"Do people really want a show about life in the West?"

"You'd be surprised."

"Well, I guess when it comes on, I can say I knew the writer."

"Maybe I'll name one of the characters after you."

I shake my head. "No way. That'd be too weird."

"Why? Because she won't measure up to you?"

God, this man. Blake knows just what to say to get me all riled up in the best way.

"Because it'd be weird to be watching someone on TV that is inspired by me. Wouldn't that be cringe-worthy?"

Blake shakes his head. "My mom is a famous actress. The number of documentaries that have had 'me' in them? You get used to it."

"And here I complain about the town's busybodies, knowing everything there is to know about me."

Swirling the wine in his glass, Blake gulps it down. "Oh, I'm sure those Hollywood hotshots have nothing on your town's busybodies. One day here, and I had pie at my door."

"They love their pies."

"See? Inspiration."

The storm rages around us as a quiet settles over the two of us. Blake's shirt clings to him. There's a slight tic in his jaw as he looks at me. Really looks at me.

"Why'd you really come over here?" I whisper.

Blake shifts off the couch, moving to kneel in front of me. His hands squeeze my knees. Those green eyes of his are dark. It sets off a fire in my belly.

"I heard you talking to Willow earlier about how you're scared of storms. I didn't want you to be alone."

Whatever worries I had of being with Blake get washed away at those words. It makes my decision for me.

Snaking my hands around his neck and into his damp hair, I latch my lips onto his.

It's even better than I remember. Firm lips take over. Each stroke of his tongue has heat gathering in my core. He guides the kiss with ease, taking what he wants while working me into a frenzy.

I want more. I want it all.

Blake's hands cup my cheeks, pulling back. Desire sits heavy in his eyes.

"Do you want this, Gemma?" Each brush of his fingers against my skin pulls me that much closer to the edge.

I nod.

"Words, Gemma. I need words."

I lick my lips, taking in every inch of his face. Green eyes. Sharp jaw line covered in scruff. The way his brown hair falls into his face.

"I want you, Blake."

Lifting me into his arms, Blake stands. All signs of playfulness are gone. The need in his eyes matches my own.

Strong fingers sink into the globes of my ass as he carries me down the hall. I lick and kiss at the pulse in his neck. He smells like rain.

Lightning flashes in the sky as Blake sets me in the center of my bed. Now that we're in here, my nerves are mixing with my need.

He settles his weight over me, his lips finding mine again. It's like they're magnets to mine. Strong hands roam down my body.

I'm a squirming mess under him, arching into him. Needing more.

"Blake…"

"What do you need?"

"I…I don't know. More?"

Another heated kiss. "More I can give you."

Blake lifts my shirt, kissing the soft skin of my stomach. His beard has me shifting below him. His hands pull down the waistband of my joggers.

His hard length is tenting his own sweats. It's causing all sorts of filthy images to fill my head.

Just because I've never had sex before doesn't mean I'm a blushing prude.

Reaching behind him, Blake pulls his T-shirt over his head and drops it beside the bed. God, his abs are drool-worthy.

"I'm glad you approve." Blake smirks down at me.

"Oh, God. Did I say that out loud?"

He hovers over me, his chest brushing against mine. "You did." His fingers fist in my shirt. "But I don't mind hearing it."

Blake nips and sucks at my lips, my jaw, my neck, before removing my shirt. My nipples are hard, ultrasensitive against the cool air.

"You are so fucking beautiful, Gemma." His breath is hot against my skin. "I don't know where I want to start."

Everywhere Blake's eyes move, I feel them. They roam over every inch of my exposed body. The lustful look in his eyes makes me bold.

Arching up, I reach behind and unsnap my bra. I do nothing else. "How about here?"

Blake drags a single finger down my chest, hooking into the front band of my bra and pulling it down. A growl escapes his lips. He reaches down, squeezing his dick in his pants.

"Gemma, what are you doing to me?" Leaning over, Blake takes a nipple between his teeth. It's like nothing I've ever felt. The scratchiness of his face against my skin sends heat coiling through me.

"Gah!" I rub my legs together, needing friction.

His mouth continues to assault my breast, alternating between nipping, sucking, and swirling his tongue around the hard peak.

My hands scratch down his back, pulling him closer. He doesn't relent, shifting his focus to the other side.

"Blake. Oh my God."

His mouth is magic.

"You like that?" The vibrations of his voice ratchet my need higher.

"Why do I feel like I could come?" It's more said to myself, but it has Blake pulling off me with a pop.

"That's not how I want you coming the first time tonight." The command in his voice is sexy.

"Then how do you want me coming?"

"The first time?" Blake asks, his eyes once again moving down my body. "The first time, I want you coming on my fingers. The second time? The second time will be on my cock."

His words increase my desire. I can't wait to feel him inside me.

"Then can you get moving?"

"Tsk, tsk. You really think I'm going to rush through this?" Warm lips come down on my stomach, licking and kissing his way south. "I plan on taking my time with you, Gemma Winchester."

"You're driving me crazy."

"Hopefully a good crazy."

Blake's fingers hook into my underwear and tug them down. I'm completely exposed to him. It's new. Exciting. Slightly anxiety-inducing.

"You're so fucking beautiful." Blake's words are calming as his lips move up my legs. "I can't wait to taste you."

"Blake," I whine.

"Patience, Gemma. I want you relaxed and ready before we get to the main show."

This. This right here is why I waited and held out for the right guy. I knew there wouldn't be the perfect guy, but I wanted the right guy.

Blake is the right guy.

"If you keep working me up, I will not be very relaxed."

He smiles against me. "We can't have that, now can we?"

Sinking a finger inside me, Blake takes me in another searing kiss. My hands find his biceps, holding on tight. He pumps his finger in and out, curling it at the right angle to send me soaring.

"Holy shit!" It's even better than the first time with Blake after the bar.

"That feel good?"

I nod. "Keep doing that."

He heeds my directions. One finger becomes two. There's a bite of pain with the pleasure as Blake draws an orgasm out of me.

Words escape me as my entire body shakes with release. Nothing has ever felt as good as this. My toes curl as my fingers scrape Blake's back, holding on to him for dear life.

Stars explode behind my eyes as Blake stills his fingers inside me. He's right there beside me, a tender smile on his face, as I come back down to earth.

"Holy shit."

"You keep saying that."

His fingers grasp my chin and turn my face toward him. His fingers—the same ones that were just inside me— paint my lips before he takes me in a heated kiss.

My pussy clenches.

It's dirty and raw and so damn good, I moan around him.

Blake takes his time, a languid kiss as his hands explore again. This time, I get my hands in on the action, pulling at the waistband of his sweats.

"Oh, no you don't." He grabs my hand and stops me.

"Why not?" I throw a little pouting lip in for good measure.

"I'm not coming until I'm inside of you."

"Then can you hurry it up?"

Blake grins down at me. "What did I tell you about that?"

I huff out a breath. "Excuse me for wanting more of that."

Kissing his way down my body, Blake's eyes stay locked on mine. "There will be plenty more of that."

His kisses are teasing as his lips land everywhere but where I truly want them. I'm going out of my mind with need when Blake stands. Shrugging out of his sweats, every hard inch of him is on display.

"It's unfair that you're that good looking."

He grabs a condom from his wallet and sets a knee on the bed.

"I could say the same to you. You look sexy as sin lying here like this. And knowing I get you all to myself?" He shakes his head. "Fuck, I don't know if I'm worthy."

My reach is hesitant, but I wrap my hand around the base of his cock.

"What are you thinking?" He grabs my jaw and forces my gaze to his.

"That I'm ready for you to be inside me." I give him a slow stroke as he steps back and opens the packet in his hand.

I'm hungry for him as Blake rolls the condom down his hard length. The perfect size.

"You ready?" He settles back over me, notching the head of his cock at my entrance.

"Yes."

I tense up as he pushes in.

"Relax. It'll make it easier."

I hold tighter as his free hand strums over my clit. He stops, letting me adjust before pushing in more. It stings and stretches as he sinks fully inside me.

I bite my lip to keep from crying out. It's uncomfortable, but not the worst kind of pain I imagined.

"You okay?" Blake peers down at me. His eyes are soft.

"I need a minute," I confess.

"Take all the time you need." Blake peppers my lips and jaw with kisses. I don't know how much time passes, but the tiniest swivel of my hips has pleasure masking the pain.

That. I want more of that.

"I'm ready."

Linking our hands together, Blake brings them next to my head. His movements are slow and steady. Out, then in. Out and in.

With each thrust, I accept him more easily. Each pass has him hitting a spot deep inside me that pushes my need higher and higher.

"You feel so good, Gem." Blake thrusts in. "So damn tight." Another thrust. "The way you're squeezing me. Fuck, it's so damn good."

"I'm close."

I never thought I'd be able to come twice in one night, but Blake is pushing me closer and closer to the edge. Blake's movements become more hurried and erratic. It only takes a few more pumps before I'm coming around him.

The orgasm before was good. This one blows it out of the water. It's almost like I black out as white-hot pleasure sears through me. It's intense, almost too much, but Blake is right there, coming. I come harder than the raging storm outside.

His head is thrown back in pleasure, the corded veins in his neck tight. I hug him to me, holding him as our heart rates slow.

"That was…" Blake starts.

"Incredible?" I finish.

A flash of lightning brightens the room.

"Give me a minute." Blake pulls out gently, accompanied by another sting of pain, before stalking off to the bathroom.

Holy shit.

Blake and I just had sex.

And it was good. Great. Mind-blowing. There are not enough words to describe it.

I never thought my first time would be like this. A bumbling mess, sure. But it was hot and tender and sexy all at the same time. I never thought I'd feel so cared for during sex, but wow. Blake is…wow.

Blake comes back, a washcloth in hand. He cleans me up before dropping it on the floor and tucking us in.

"How do you feel?" Pulling me into his arms, his lips find my shoulder.

I turn, peering up into his green eyes. "I'll let you know when I come back down to earth."

The storm quiets around us as we drift off to sleep.

The perfect way to pass the storm.

Chapter Fourteen

BLAKE

Stirring beside me wakes me up. This bed is way more comfortable than the one I've been sleeping on. Mainly because of the woman beside me.

Gray skies are still shrouded in rain. Trees are swaying with the wind. It howls around us. But the cabin is cozy.

Gemma is still fast asleep. Her lips are parted and her hair is a mess around her.

Holy shit.

I still can't believe last night happened.

Every minute was perfect. She was perfect.

Letting her sleep, I get up and use the bathroom before pulling on my sweats and heading into the kitchen.

I didn't pay much attention to Gemma's cabin last time I was here. It's exactly as I'd expect from her.

Warm and welcoming. Pictures of the mountains and horses decorate the walls. Flannel blankets are strewn over the couch that sits in front of the fireplace. The living room overlooks the back part of the ranch, the Tetons in the distance.

Pictures of her family line the mantel.

It even smells like her. Like fresh mountain air and vanilla.

I had no expectations when I came over here last night. With the storm raging, I was worried about her. I heard her conversation with Willow. I didn't want her to be alone.

Every day spent here in Dixon is one I want to spend with her.

Digging in the fridge, I pull out a container of eggs and get to work. The coffee is easy enough to find and start.

"I thought I smelled something cooking."

Gemma comes into the kitchen, wearing only my T-shirt.

Fuck. Why does it look so damn good on her? I want to peel it off her and have her for breakfast.

"Pretty basic. Scrambled eggs are hard to screw up."

"No one's ever made me breakfast before."

Gemma steps behind me, wrapping her arms around me.

"How do you feel this morning?"

"Like I want to do that again." She kisses my back before hopping onto the counter. I don't miss the wince as she sits down.

"Maybe you might want to wait a bit."

Reaching over, she grabs the pot of coffee and pours herself a cup.

"You can't tell me no now. Not when it was that good."

Taking the eggs off the heat, I step between her legs. "Only good?"

She sips on her coffee. "I don't think you need me to inflate your ego."

I push her legs apart and grab the mug from her, taking my own sip. "Not inflating my ego if I want to make sure your first time was more than good."

Her hands land on my bare chest. It has my dick stirring in my pants. I can't seem to get enough of this woman's touch.

"Are first times always that good?" she asks quietly.

"Mine was terrible."

"Really?"

I nod. "I told you the story. It scarred both of us, being in the news like that, so we waited awhile before doing it again. Even the second time wasn't great."

"Glad I didn't have that then."

I laugh, wrapping my arms around her. "I'm glad I'm more experienced now so you didn't have to suffer like I did." I kiss her neck. I can't be with her and not kiss her.

She's addicting.

"I don't think I could have asked for anything more perfect," she confesses.

I take another kiss. This woman is slowly unraveling every part of my closed-off heart.

"I'm really glad I had this proposal."

"You sure you know what you're getting yourself into?"

Dragging a finger down my chest, I notice the blush that creeps up her skin.

"What am I getting myself into?" I stop her hand and tip her face up to look at me.

"Give me a minute."

She hops off the counter, and I watch her retreat.

Grabbing the eggs off the stove, I divvy them between two plates and walk to the table. When Gemma returns, she's thrown my sweatshirt on over her.

She's swimming in it. It's then I notice the piece of paper in her hand.

"What's that?"

"You want the true ranch experience? Then I want the true sex experience."

"Okay…" I trail off, not sure where she's going with this.

"I have a list."

I shift, trying to get my dick to calm down. He is all of a sudden very interested in this conversation.

"Can I see it?"

Her cheeks are red as she hands over the list.

Gemma's Sexual Awakening

THAT TITLE alone has me ready to throw her down on this table and start with whatever is on this list. She's casual, sitting next to me, eating her eggs.

My eyes skim down the list.

Blow jobs and/or 69-ing
Costumes
Shower sex
Kitchen sex
Sex in the bed of a truck
Blindfold and tied up
Get eaten out
Food eaten off me
Anal sex
No talking sex

"NO TALKING?" I question.

She nods, shoveling a forkful of eggs into her mouth.

"It was on a show I saw. They didn't talk, and it heightened the experience for both of them."

"Fuck, Gemma."

"What? Is it not doable?" She grabs the list out of my hand and skims it again.

"Oh, it's doable, alright."

"Then what's the problem?"

I grab her hand, and she drops the list. I take her around the waist and pull her into my lap, where I let her feel my very obvious response to her list.

"Oh."

"Yeah, fucking oh."

I drag my nose up the length of her neck.

"So doable?" She rolls her hips over my lap.

"You're killing me."

"Then we're doing this."

Gemma's hands sink into my hair, tilting my head back to gaze into her eyes. There's no hesitation. They have the confidence of a woman who knows exactly what she wants.

Me.

"Then we're doing this."

A sly smile paints her face. "Should we shake on it?"

Standing, I take her in my arms and spread her out on the table.

"Oh, I have a much better idea than that."

Chapter Fifteen

"Why are we shopping again?" I flip through another rack in Layla's store.

"Because, I need a cute top for a date tonight." Ivy pulls out a light pink top, holds it up to her, then puts it back.

"And who is this date with? Why haven't I heard about it before now?"

Ivy rolls her eyes. "I'm telling you now. And I like this guy, so I didn't want to jinx it."

"Do I know him?"

"What did I just tell you?" Ivy turns her amber eyes on me.

"Sorry."

Ivy grabs a few shirts from a table, adding them to the growing pile of lingerie and jeans in her arms, before grabbing my hand and leading me to the back of the store. The dressing rooms are nothing short of fabulous.

Oversized pink chairs line one wall while a three-way mirror sits next to them. An old chandelier hangs from the ceiling, and two large dressing rooms take up the rest of the space.

It's everything you would want when trying on clothes.

"Where are you two going tonight?"

"I don't know yet."

"Then how do you know what you should be getting?"

"Your logic has no place here, Gem." Ivy brushes off my question as she pulls me into the dressing room behind her.

"Right."

Ivy doesn't see my smile as she yanks her top over her head.

"How are things going with that writer boy of yours?"

"They're going just fine."

"Fine?" Ivy throws her hands down, stuck in the confines of her top. Her eyes meet mine in the mirror. "That storm would have been the perfect opportunity to wander over to Blake's cabin and 'snuggle.'"

This time, Ivy doesn't miss my face.

"What was that?"

"What was what?"

Crap. There's no playing this off.

"Did something happen?" Her face widens in shock. "Have you been holding out on me this whole time?"

"We've been out for an hour, Ivy."

"And that's an hour too long if something happened!" She throws off her top and pulls on the one she brought in with her to try on. "Did something happen?"

I nod.

"Oh my God!" she shrieks.

I shush her. "I don't think everyone in the store heard you."

"What happened?" Her voice softens, but only a little.

I bite the corner of my mouth. "Everything."

"Oh my God!" Ivy's back to shrieking.

"Will you please keep it down?"

"That's your own fault for telling me when we're shopping."

"Ugh, fine." I finger the lacy cup of the bra that's hanging in the dressing room. "Speaking of, why are we looking for lingerie? I thought you needed a new top for the date."

It still astounds me that my big sister is this creative. I don't have a creative bone in my body.

"Never hurts to look nice underneath too." She pulls a shirt down over her head. It's one of Layla's newest designs. It's a simple nude tank with a floral overlay. Probably one of the most beautiful things I've seen.

"Are you listening to me?" Ivy turns in the mirror, admiring the top. "Or did Blake take your brains too?"

"Stop it." I drop into the chair in the oversized dressing room. "Is this really what you want to talk about right now?"

"Yes."

"Only if you keep your voice down."

"You two doing okay in here?" Layla's voice sounds from over the door.

"Fine!" I answer before Ivy can.

"Be out in a second," Ivy calls out. Stripping out of the top, Ivy puts on what she was wearing earlier and hangs the top back up.

"All set."

"That's it?" I look at the pile on the bench.

"This is it." She holds out the top on the hanger. "It will drive my man crazy."

Grabbing the matching bra and underwear, I follow her out of the dressing room. She stacks the nos on the go-back table. Before I can put the sexy lingerie on the rack again, Ivy stalls me.

"You keep eyeing this. You need to get it."

Ivy thrusts the lacy lingerie set into my hands. The light blue material is see-through, with gold vines wrapping over the material. It's stunning.

"I don't know what I'd do with this."

"Gem. Wear it for that sexy new man of yours. He sees you in that?" She eyes me up and down. "He won't know what to do with himself."

"What's this about a new man?" Layla comes up behind us.

"Geez, Layla. Do you always sneak up on customers like this?"

"Only the ones I'm related to. And only when I hear something about a new man."

"There's no—"

"She's got a man."

"Ivy!"

"Gemma! Why didn't you tell me?"

"I—"

Layla holds up a finger, stopping me. "This calls for wine."

Marching over to the front of the store, she tells the woman working the front desk—someone she went to high school with—that she'll be a few minutes and then calls us to the back room.

It's an explosion of fabric and mannequins. Half-completed pieces hang from the bodies. From what's on them, I already know next season is going to be even better for Layla.

"Now, I want the details."

Layla grabs a bottle of open wine. Popping the top, she fills three glasses.

"She's been a touch scarce on them," Ivy tells her matter-of-factly.

"Only because you didn't give me a chance."

Two sets of eyes stare back at me. "Now's your chance, Gem."

Sometimes Layla reminds me so much of my mother, it's scary.

"Blake and I…"

"Did the horizontal tango? Knocked boots? Bumped uglies?"

I choke over my wine. "Why is it called bumping uglies? There is nothing ugly about that man."

It takes me a minute to realize what I've told them, but both of their eyes widen.

"I can't believe you finally gave it up!"

"It's not like it was a conscious choice I was making. I just couldn't find someone I liked to even want to date. Why would I give it up to them?"

"Ignoring that," Layla circles her hand in the air in a silent request for me to continue. "What's Blake like?

The thought of him has every part of my body tingling from the memories of what he did to me.

"He's smart. And sexy. And fun."

"Good for you for not settling." I don't miss the pain that flashes in Layla's eyes. She's had a rough go of it since her divorce.

"It's just…"

"Just what?" Ivy asks, sipping on her wine.

"How long is he staying for? He keeps saying a few weeks. But his life is back in LA."

"Gemma—"

"Let me," Layla cuts Ivy off. "I am the first person to tell you that you should be careful. I settled and now look at me. I'm divorced before the age of thirty."

Every time Layla mentions her divorce, it make me sad for her. My big sister is one of my favorite people in the world, and her divorce broke her. It's taken her years to get back to some semblance of who she used to be.

"Instead of playing it safe for once"—she pauses—"do the reckless thing."

I sip on my wine. "I don't know if I've ever been reckless in my life."

Layla smiles at me. "There's a first time for everything. Have fun. Enjoy yourself with this guy who can teach you a thing or two."

I laugh, thinking about the list.

Oh yeah. There will definitely be some learning all right.

"And when he leaves?"

Ivy reaches across the table, clasping my arm. "Then that's why you have us."

I was so wrapped up in the moment with Blake, that I didn't stop to think about what his leaving might do to me.

Layla's right. I should enjoy it. I so rarely do things for myself. I'm always putting the ranch first.

And should my heart get broken?

Well, I guess I have these two women I can lean on.

Chapter Sixteen

BLAKE

"**D**o I really have to wear this?"

Gemma gives me an annoyed look. I'd be miffed if she wasn't so damn cute.

"By all means, wear regular shoes and pants. Makes no difference to me if you're sopping wet to your balls."

I snort, choking around the sip of coffee I just had.

"Jesus, Gemma. Warn a guy next time."

The truck rumbles down the road, closer to the river. After that storm blew through, it's like life exploded out here. Trees are greening from the mountains as far as the eye can see, mixed in with wildflowers. It's nothing you see in LA, that's for sure.

"You ready for this?" Gemma pulls the truck over into a pullout next to the river.

"As long as you show me how."

Opening the door, Gemma hops out of the truck and I follow.

"You'll get the hang of it."

Gemma grabs a tackle box out of the bed of the truck

along with two fishing poles. I follow her down to a shallow part of the river.

I didn't have the first clue what Gemma would show me about western life. I had pretty limited ideas to be honest.

Even though I've never been fishing before, I can't say I mind spending the day with Gemma.

The burbling river sparkles in the sun. Everything about this place continues to blow me away. When I got here, I figured I'd be stuck in my room for twelve hours a day trying to find my muse.

Turns out my muse looks pretty sexy in fishing gear.

"Are you paying attention?" Gemma asks.

"Sorry. My teacher is looking pretty sexy right now, and it's a distraction."

She leans up, giving me a quick peck before shoving a fishing rod in my hand. "A for smoothness, but don't think I'm letting you off easy."

"Teach me how to be one with the fish, Miss Winchester."

She baits our hooks and demonstrates the movement. "You'll get the hang of it. Try a few times without the pole."

I swing my arm back and forth a few times as she corrects my moves. "Like that?"

"Not as much wrist. You want to arc your arm more so the line goes farther out. You don't want to drop it right in front of you."

This time, after I get it right, she hands me the pole. "Cast over there." She points to a clump of trees. "The fish like it."

I follow her lead, wading farther into the water and casting my line.

"What do we do now?"

"We wait."

"What if the fish don't bite?"

She shrugs a shoulder like it isn't a big deal. "Then the fish don't bite."

"I don't know if I see the appeal in this."

"It's peaceful. I could spend hours out here and not see another soul."

"Do you usually come out here by yourself?"

"Every once in a while. Sometimes Gramps comes with me, but I enjoy floating down the river on my own."

I eye her as she recasts her line. She instructs me to do the same.

"You surprise me."

"How?" She turns her attention to me, not even realizing that she's messing with her line as she does. This is like second nature to her.

"You're outdoorsy. You're a badass, out here casting lines like it's no big deal. It's pretty cool."

"Wait until you see me on a horse."

"I can't wait."

"You'll love it."

"You know, maybe I could have my characters out here fishing on horses."

Gemma bursts out laughing.

"What? It's not that crazy of an idea."

Gemma shakes her head. "No self-respecting fisherman would be caught dead on a horse." She wades closer to me. "How in the world are you going to catch the fish once you get him?"

I throw my hands up awkwardly with the fishing pole in my hand. "Okay, fine. Point proven."

She beams back at me as I recast a perfect line. "You want the true western experience. I have to make sure it's authentic for you."

"What else is going to be in my western experience?"

"We've already done archery."

"Yeah, where a seven-year-old kicked my ass," I grumble.

"I can always teach you more. There's still horseback riding. The chef's tasting. Maybe even a canoe trip," Gemma lists off.

"As long as you're my guide."

We've shifted closer to one another as we wait for the fish to bite.

She's right. This really is relaxing. People in the city would hate this—standing still and waiting with no cell reception.

"I want to do something like this." Gemma doesn't look at me.

"Something like what? Fishing?"

She casts her line again. "A program like this. We send so much business out to other companies to give people a true western experience. Why can't we do one?"

"Would you be in charge of it?"

Her face is hidden below the wide brim of her hat. "I want to be. I love working at the ranch. But I want to do more than just be the check-in girl. I love being outdoors."

"So start one."

"I wish it were that easy."

"Why isn't it?"

This time, Gemma turns to face me. She looks like she's figuring out how much to tell me. "I don't want to rock the boat."

"I've met your family. I don't know why they would say no."

Gemma laughs, not her usual cheerful laugh. This one has a sadness to it I'm not used to from her.

"I'm the baby of the family. I get coddled and looked

over a lot." She holds a hand up, almost horrified at what she just said. "Not that I don't love them. I do. But now, with Logan needing help, it's like no one wants to change the status quo in case it sends him off the deep end."

"Yeah, but what you're doing is for the good of the ranch. I'd sign up to have you teach me the ways of the West."

This pulls a smile out of her. "I like that you're my guinea pig."

I dip down, capturing her lips in a sweet kiss. "Guinea pig, you say? Does that make you my—"

She slaps a hand over my mouth. "If you say you're my sex guinea pig, I'm going to throw you down river and leave you for the fish."

Laughter erupts out of me. "You're one of a kind, Gemma Winchester."

"I can't take you anywhere." This time, her laugh is happy. It washes over me and fills in all the cracks. I could hear it every day for the rest of my life and it still wouldn't be enough.

When did I become so far gone for her?

The pole tugs in my hand, my line going ramrod straight. "Holy shit! I've got a bite!"

Gemma reels her line in and catches my hand.

"Bring him in slow and steady. Don't pull."

Her hands guide my movements as the line gets shorter and shorter. The fish is squirming in the water as Gemma grabs a net to bring him in. She pulls the hook out of his mouth.

"He's huge!"

Gemma eyes me before looking down into the net. "Men. Always exaggerating how big something is."

"He has to be a foot long!"

Gemma holds the net out to me. Inches are marked on the inside padding.

Four inches.

"No way. He has to be bigger than that."

Gemma reaches in with one hand and brings him out. "Really?"

He's the size of her hand. "Okay, fine. But he looked bigger in the water."

"If you want to tell everyone back home that you caught a foot-long trout, I won't stop you. I'll know you're full of shit, but they can be impressed with your newfound fishing skills."

I feign hurt. "Way to cut a man down, Gemma."

"You want to hold him?" She extends her hand to me. The fish is gaping.

"Eww, no."

"C'mon. Don't be such a baby. You can even kiss him if you want."

My face screws up in disgust. I can't help it. Who would want to kiss a fish?

"No, thanks."

"It's not bad." Gemma gives him a light peck on the lips before holding him out to me.

"That's disgusting."

"Are you sure?" She pushes him even closer to me.

"Oh God!" I jump back, landing squarely on my ass.

She's laughing at me as she sets the fish down in the river and he swims away.

"We're not going to eat him?"

Gemma shakes her head. "No. It'd be wasteful."

"We don't even get to enjoy the fruits of my hard work?"

Gemma's staring down at me, her hands on her hips.

She looks fucking adorable in her hat and waders. "You okay down there?"

"I'm glad I'm wearing the waders now."

"I'm sorry, was there a 'Gemma is right' in there?" She cups her hand next to her ear.

"Are you always like this?" I grumble.

Gemma reaches a hand out to help me up, but I pull her down next to me.

"Hey!"

"You're insufferable."

I tilt the brim of her hat up. Her cheeks have picked up a bit of color in the sun. Oversized waders shouldn't be as sexy as they are, but Gemma is stunning. I love getting to see her in her element like this.

I lean in closer.

"Are you sure you want to kiss me?"

She puckers up like the fish she just threw back into the river.

"You think the fish scare me?"

"Umm, yes." There's a playful gleam in her eyes.

I don't think twice.

I kiss her.

Fishy lips and all.

Chapter Seventeen

GEMMA

"Are you sure you don't want to be doing this in the kitchen?" Chef Wayne asks again. "The whole point of the chef's table is doing it in the kitchen, where I can tell you about each course."

As I load the last containers into the bag, I glance up at him and smile. "I know all about these meals. I'd rather do it in the comfort of Blake's cabin."

He shakes his head at me. "Only because it's you, Gemma, will I allow it. I hope we don't get a critical review for this."

"Now Wayne,"—I cross my arms and pin him with a glare—"do you really think my guest of honor will give you a bad review?"

"If my quail lollipops aren't served at the right temperature, then yes."

I drop a kiss on his wrinkly cheek. "It'll be fine."

And if it's not? I can think of multiple ways to distract Blake that will be more fun.

"And you have the good wine?"

"The Domaine Tortochot Burgundy. I have the good wine, Wayne. Now relax."

"Easy for you to say when you don't have to prepare dinner for thirty guests."

"Just another Wednesday night for you." I wink at him as I head out the door and away from the heavenly scents of his amazing dishes cooking in the kitchen.

One of my favorite parts about the ranch is our ever-expanding menu. We were lucky to find Chef Wayne. He came from a small beach town in Florida and has revolutionized our restaurant.

People come from all over to experience his outlandish cuisine.

Want to try rattlesnake sausage? We have it.

Bison tenderloin? You'll never want any other kind ever again.

By the time I get to Blake's cabin, he's waiting for me on the porch.

My steps stutter as I take him in. He looks relaxed—far different from the tightly wound Blake when he arrived.

His shirt sleeves are rolled up and jeans hug his thighs.

But the real kicker?

The wide cowboy hat resting on his head.

Lord help me, but I don't know if I'll ever be able to tell this man no.

Because he looks like a dream come to life as he smiles at me.

"Looking pretty good there, cowboy."

I pause as my foot hits the top step.

"What do you think? I fit right in, right?" He stands, doing a twirl for good measure.

"They'll be inducting you as a Dixonite tomorrow."

"What's the ceremony involve?" Blake holds out his hand, pulling me up to him.

"You have to lasso a cow." I keep my face straight.

"Damn. Guess I'm going to need some more practice then."

"Guess so."

Blake hauls me in, tipping his hat up. "Nice to see you, little lady."

I can't help it. Laughter bursts out of me. "Now I know you bought that hat down at Cowboy Joe's. He's the only one who would give you a line as cheesy as that to use."

Blake plucks the hat off his head and drops it on mine. "Guess I'll let you be the cowgirl tonight then."

I don't miss the heat in his eyes as he stares down at me. I feel it everywhere. Tipping the hat back, I take his lips in a heated kiss. I want Blake to feel everything I'm feeling.

I never knew things could be like this with a man. The few guys I dated in high school and college don't hold a candle to Blake.

One look. One touch from this man and I'm crazy with need. He's awakened a desire in me I never knew I could feel.

All too soon, Blake steps back.

"As much as I'd like to keep doing this, whatever you have in that bag smells incredible."

I take a minute to get my bearings.

"Right. Eat. Dinner."

"Nice job on using your words, Gemma," Blake jokes.

I smack him on the chest and head inside his small cabin. All the guest cabins are what I call cowboy chic. Black-and-white portraits from the ranch throughout the years cover the walls. An old saddle hangs above the fireplace. The cozy scents of teakwood and tobacco give it a homey feel.

Setting the bag down on the kitchen counter, I shoo

Blake away. "Grab two glasses for the wine while I get this set up."

I pass the bottle of wine to Blake as I take the containers out of the bag. Plucking each lid off, the heavenly scents of dinner hit me.

Chef Wayne really is a renaissance cook.

I make quick work of plating all the courses that were made and set it out on the table.

"Wow. This looks incredible." Blake comes back into the kitchen with two full glasses of red wine.

"The chef's tasting menu in the comfort of your own cabin."

I take the proffered glass of wine from Blake.

"Are we having it here so I can kiss you?"

"One of the reasons." I press a kiss to the corner of his mouth. "But Chef Wayne is nosey. He and Gramps love sitting around before dinner with some of Peter's vodka and gossiping about what's going on at the ranch."

A look of understanding washes over his face. "And you don't want them gossiping about us?"

"Not at all. My siblings are already doing enough of that. The entire town, really."

"Guess I'm something of a hot commodity."

"That you are."

Placing a hand on my hip, Blake spins me and moves us toward the table. He pulls out my seat and I sit before he takes the seat next to me.

"Where do we start?"

I hold my glass up in a toast. "To the chef's tasting."

"The chef's tasting."

We clink glasses and sip on the exquisite wine.

I grab the small card that Chef Wayne put in the bag. "I have very strict instructions about serving the meal in the proper order."

Blake takes the card from my hand and skims over it. "Holy shit. This sounds delicious."

I smile and put the first dish on his plate. "You're in a for a treat. Chef Wayne is amazing."

"Mexican summer squash soup." Blake peers down at the bowl in front of him, topped off with slices of avocado, cotija cheese, and cilantro. "This is the first course?"

"Yes." I dip my spoon into the bowl and blow. The first bite is delicious—as I knew it would be.

"Damn. This is terrific."

I smile. "Just you wait."

"Oh, I can't imagine how good everything else is. Those roasted quail lollipops sound weird, but oddly delicious."

"That's a great way to describe the food. We try to locally source as much of the food as possible."

"Well, it's fucking incredible." Blake takes the last bite of his soup. "I never knew there'd be food like this here."

I hand Blake the small plate of appetizers. "Are these the quail pops?"

"Mm-hmm. And rattlesnake sausage bites."

"Rattlesnake?" This time, Blake looks disgusted. "As in the snake."

I plop two onto his plate with the accompanying sauce. "Please withhold all judgment until you try them."

Blake takes a bite and chews quietly. "Okay, why is this so good?"

"Because it is." I lean over and bite the remaining piece out of his hands.

"Hey! I wanted that."

I smile around the bite. "Sorry. Too slow."

"I feel like I need to punish you."

"Oh, yeah?" I cross my legs and turn toward him. "What would that entail?"

Blake walks his fingers up my leg. Each soft caress has my stomach exploding with butterflies.

"Oh, I think the punishment would be keeping the specifics to myself and letting you stew."

He pulls his hand away and I miss the heat of his touch. "That's just mean."

"Payback." Blake grabs the last quail appetizer and pops it into his mouth. "Now, tell me about the main courses."

"Chef made two main courses for us. We have seared Idaho steelhead trout—"

"You said we couldn't eat it," Blake complains.

"When we're fishing like that, no. It'd be wasteful. But they caught these sustainably, so we're not hurting them."

Blake points to the dish now on his plate. "But this could've been the trout I caught?"

"If you want to tell yourself that, then he's the fish you caught."

He looks so proud of himself. "Then I definitely caught this fish."

"The second dish," I say as I circle back, "is herb-crusted elk loin with grilled asparagus."

Blake spears a small bite of the elk and chews. "I don't think I've ever had something this flavorful before."

"Really? You lived in Paris." I cut off a piece of the fish and pop it in my mouth.

"Where my major food groups consisted of pasta and pastries. I was too young to appreciate it and haven't been back since."

"Well, I'm glad I can teach you a thing or two."

"You are, Gemma. You are."

We eat the main courses in companionable silence. Even having worked at the ranch since I was young, I've never really had the chance to experience the chef's tasting in its full grandeur. Sure, I always have a meal here or there when I'm working, but nothing this extravagant.

Getting to experience it for the first time with Blake? It's special.

"I don't know if I have room for dessert." Blake sips on his wine. "I'm stuffed."

"You'll think twice once you see it."

I open the last dish. "Dessert is blackberry crisp with a strawberry whipped cream."

Blake moves in close, dragging his nose up the length of my neck. "Think we can save some of that whipped cream for later?"

"Oh, yeah?"

Blake tugs my earlobe between his teeth. "I'm suddenly famished and need to lick it off every part of you."

I gulp down the rest of my wine.

"Then what are you waiting for?"

Chapter Eighteen

GEMMA

Blake's hot on my heels as I run into the bedroom. He grabs me from behind as we fall onto the bed. Our lips lock in a passionate kiss. Blake's weight settles over me as he takes control. My hands slide under his shirt, fingering each ab.

I swallow the growl as his lips kiss a path down my jaw. Nipping at my ear. Licking down my neck. I want more. I want everything with Blake tonight.

Whipped cream and all.

"Want to try to knock off two bullet points from your list tonight?" Blake asks, hovering over me.

"And what part is that?"

Rocking back onto his heels, Blake undoes the clasp on his belt. He pulls it out slowly. Oh so slowly.

"What about tying you up?"

"Tying me up?" I echo, gulping down the nerves that are now threatening to burst free.

Blake nods. "We don't have to if you don't want to."

"No!" My voice is a little too loud, even to my own ears. "I mean, I want to."

"Do you trust me?"

"I trust you."

"Then you want to try it?"

My eyes lock onto Blake's. They're so dark, they're the color of pine trees. But beneath all that heat is a tenderness. Telling me to take this leap with him.

"Okay."

"Safe word is—"

"We need a safe word?"

"Yes." Blake's voice is firm. "Strawberry."

"You want me to say strawberry if I want you to stop?"

"Say it and I stop right away."

"Strawberry. Got it." My lips quirk up in the barest hint of a smile.

Grabbing the back of his shirt, Blake tugs it over his head and drops it next to the bed. I don't know if I'll ever get tired of drinking him in. Every muscle. Every dip and curve. I could stare at it every day for the rest of my life and it wouldn't be enough.

Leaning over me, Blake takes both my hands in his and hauls them up the bed. Strong hands wrap the leather belt around my wrists. It's tight, but not uncomfortable since they're not tied to the bed.

"That good?"

I nod. "Yes."

"Good."

One hand holds my locked wrists in place while the other starts to undo the buttons on my shirt. Each brush of his fingertips against my skin is setting me on fire.

I never knew I could feel desire like this. Every part of my body knows exactly where Blake is. It's like my cells are all racing to feel his touch.

As he gets to the final button, Blake pulls the sides of my shirt apart, revealing what's underneath.

One hand scrubs over his face while the other squeezes his cock.

"What's this?" Blake's eyes trail over the thin material covering my breast.

"Just a little something I picked up."

I've never worn anything this nice—this fancy—before. The look in Blake's eyes right now makes me happy Ivy and Layla forced me to buy it.

Very happy.

And based on his current reaction, he's very happy too.

His eyes hold a reverence to them as he gazes at me. My nipples tighten under his gaze.

"You are the sexiest fucking thing I've ever seen, Gemma. I want to rip this right off of you."

"You'd better not."

"No, I don't think so." His finger trails over the heaving skin that's exposed on my right breast. "I want to see you in this again."

Blake's smile is sultry as he leans over me, flattening his tongue over the sheer material. It's like a shot of fire right to my core. Everything this man does to me drives me wild.

He does it again, licking the tight bud again and again. I want to reach to him. Cling to him so his mouth stays right where I want it.

"That feels so good." Something about the fabric rubbing against my nipple as Blake works me over is driving my need higher and higher.

"It's about to feel even better."

Unhooking the front clasp of my bra, Blake pushes it to the side, exposing my chest. A coolness then hits one nipple.

Whipped cream. Blake drags his finger through the cream, pulling it across my chest. It's almost a balm to my overheated skin.

Blake flicks his tongue through the mess, connecting with my nipple.

"Oh my God!" I shout. "That feels so good."

"Only good?" Blake does it again, this time swirling his tongue around the tight bud.

Words escape me. Strong hands hold me down as he slowly—deliberately—winds me up, licking every drop off of me.

"You taste so good." His mouth crashes to mine. It's cool as our tongues connect, the sweetness of the strawberry lingering there. I arch into his touch, my chest brushing against his. It's like a rocket, sending me even closer to release.

Blake undoes the button on my jeans, sliding the zipper down. Each snick of the zipper echoes around the quiet room. Tugging each leg off, Blake tosses the denim to the side.

I can't imagine how I look. Bra and shirt hanging wide open, in only a skimpy pair of underwear with my hands tied up over my head.

Yet, somehow, I've never felt sexier than I do right now.

I don't know what it is about Blake, but he makes me feel safe. He blew into my life, completely unexpected. Like I can do whatever I want with him and he won't judge me. I've never felt that before.

Maybe that's why I trusted him with the list. With my body. With everything.

"Still doing okay, Gem?"

I nod.

"Words, please."

"Yes," I whine.

"Good girl."

Blake kisses his way up my leg, lips ghosting over where

I want to feel him most. My head is thrown back. I'm aching, dripping wet. He's driving me crazy.

His lips move back down my thigh before sliding the skimpy material down my legs.

"This is going to be good."

My eyes fly open. The cool cream lands on my buzzing skin, just above my pussy. Blake's smile is sinful as his tongue darts out, dragging the white cream lower, swirling it around my clit.

"Holy shit!" I practically fly off the bed.

That tongue of his is magic. Swirling and licking. Flicking and sucking.

Pure magic.

Blake sinks a finger inside my tight pussy. His tongue and finger stroke me, as I grind down on him. I can't get enough of him on me.

I shift, staring down at him. His eyes are locked on mine, whipped cream covering his mouth. The sight of him eating me out makes me come undone.

It's like an out-of-body experience. Every cell is alive, pulsing through me as I come. It's the most intense feeling. My toes curl. My fingers dig into my palms. My scream is stifled because I can't seem to find my voice.

I don't know how much time has passed, but Blake is there, staring down at me like he wants to eat me. Not that he just didn't, but again. Like the first time wasn't enough.

My release glistens on his lips. A tiny bit of whipped cream sticks to the corner of his mouth.

"That was fucking hot."

"Oh yeah?" My voice is breathless.

Blake's thumb trails over my lips. "Want a taste?"

I don't answer, leaning up and taking his lips in a kiss.

It's sinful. Dirty. Depraved.

I suck up every taste of my release—mixed with the strawberry whipped cream—from him.

"You ready for more?"

"More?"

I don't just want more with Blake. I want it all.

Standing, Blake shoves his jeans and boxer briefs down. His cock is leaking, hard and long.

I lick my lips. "I want to taste it."

"You don't have to."

He takes a step closer, dropping a knee onto the bed.

"I know. But I want to."

"Because it's on the list?" Blake asks.

I shake my head. "Because I want to."

"You might want to get more comfortable."

Blake shifts the pillows around, giving me a better angle.

"Go slow. And you can stop anytime you want."

"I know the safe word," I tell him. My voice is strong. I want my own taste of Blake.

Stroking my cheek, Blake moves his cock closer to my lips. It's bigger this close up.

"Wait."

"You okay?" He pulls back immediately.

"Whipped cream."

"We don't have to do that this time, Gem."

"Blake, I want to. Let me. Please."

"Okay." Grabbing the container, Blake holds it out to me. It's awkward with my hands still tied together, but I coat my fingers and then take his dick in hand.

"Shit," Blake hisses.

"Is this okay?"

"Yeah." The muscles in his neck are strained. "I'll tell you if I don't like anything, but I guarantee you I'll like whatever you do."

Blake's dick twitches as I spread the cool cream along his velvety length. It's hard and soft at the same time.

And I love seeing just how hard I make him.

Me.

Gemma Winchester.

I guide him closer to my lips, taking a tentative lick.

"Like that." Blake's voice is gravelly.

My still-tied hands hold the base of his dick as I guide him into my mouth, taking the head in. It's a weird sensation, but I'm more than eager.

Each circle of my tongue has me taking a bit more in. The sweetness and salt are exploding on my tongue together. It's a heady sensation.

I try to take more of him, but gag slightly and pull back.

"You okay?" Blake strokes my chin.

I nod, taking a breath before taking him back in my mouth. I don't take him all the way to the back of my throat, but greedily suck as much of him as I can. Seeing how worked up Blake is keeps me going. Licking. Sucking. Enjoying the feel of his heavy cock on my tongue.

"Shit. Stop."

"What's wrong?" I pull off him completely. I know my skills in this area are lacking, but I thought I was doing a good job.

"I don't want to come in your mouth."

"Oh." It's hard to fight the smile that spreads across my face as Blake grabs the condom from the nightstand and rolls it on.

Taking my hands in his, Blake guides me back into the center of the bed and settles over me. Lining himself up, he sinks inside, inch by inch. I'm still dripping after my last release. It lets me take him just a bit easier than last time. There's still the bite of pain, but not as bad as last time.

The overwhelming pleasure overrides any pain.

Blake's hips swivel, moving slowly. Abs flex. Biceps tighten as he moves. It's intoxicating to watch him as he takes his own pleasure from me.

I meet him, thrust for thrust.

"I'm so close, Blake. So close."

"Me too. Fuck, Gemma. That blow job was so hot." He thrusts harder. "I want to do that again." Thrust. "Seeing that pretty little mouth of yours taking my dick is so fucking hot."

"I want to do it again," I tell him.

He links our hands as best he can, his forehead kissing mine. Heat swirls around us, the air electric. So hot, one spark could ignite it.

It only takes a few more thrusts before Blake is sending me flying again. He comes on a roar, pumping into me through his own orgasm. It draws out my own.

"Holy shit," Blake mutters.

Holy shit is right. I never thought sex could be this good. A vibrator only gets one so far.

Blake? Blake has quite possibly ruined me for every other man on the planet.

Two earth-shattering orgasms in one night is going to be hard for anyone to compare to.

Not that I'm thinking about anyone else right now.

I want the man who is unbinding my wrists with care. Kissing them. Rubbing away the red spots before shucking the rest of my clothes and tucking me into his arms.

I settle with a sigh.

"You okay?"

I smile against Blake's chest, his fingers combing through my hair. "Better than okay."

"It's not the back of a pickup truck…"

I smile at him. "It'll do."

"I think I might need to start making a list of my own."

"I would gladly help you with that."

"I've found you to be a very good student, Gem."

"Oh, yeah?" I shift, resting my chin on my chest and staring into those hazy green eyes of his. He's as spent as I am.

"Very. A+."

"Well, you aren't the only one who learned something tonight."

"What did you learn?" Blake squeezes me to him. "That I have mad skills?"

"Oh my God. That was terrible!" I shove at his chest, covering my mouth as laughter breaks free.

"What did you learn then?" Blake nuzzles his face into my neck, nipping at the soft skin there.

"I don't think I'll ever look at whipped cream the same way again."

Chapter Nineteen

BLAKE

"Hey you."

Gemma's voice pulls me away from the furious typing on my keyboard. She looks positively well-loved from last night. With only my T-shirt covering her, the bite marks on her legs are obvious.

"How you feeling this morning?" Grabbing her hand, I pull her down on the couch next to me.

"Like I have a newfound appreciation for strawberry whipped cream."

"Mmm." I press a sweet kiss onto her lips. "You and me both."

"What are you working on?"

I twist my laptop to show her the screen. "An idea came to me for a family dinner."

"I hope it doesn't involve the things we did." There's a cheeky glimmer in her eye.

I nip at her bottom lip. "That's not going in the story. That memory will be only for me."

"Good." Gemma's hand rests on my bare abs. I could get used to mornings like this. "Can I read it?"

"It's a rough draft."

"So that's a no?" She quirks a brow in my direction.

"It's a 'be gentle' because it hasn't been sent to the studio to be torn to pieces yet."

"That doesn't sound like fun."

I laugh. "Believe me, it's an existential crisis every time I send it off."

Gemma grabs my laptop and hauls it into her lap. I watch as her eyes rove over the screen. Her face gives nothing away.

The farther along she reads, the deeper the furrow in her brow gets. When she cocks her head to the side, I can't take it anymore.

"What's wrong with it?"

"What?" She looks up at me like she forgot I was in the room.

"You have a face." I rub a finger between her brows.

"It's not my script…"

"But?"

"It's just, family dinners aren't this formal."

"What?" I grab the laptop back and look at my words.

"I know you don't have any siblings, but it's usually not this quiet."

"There'll be background noise when they film it."

"But it doesn't have the chaos of a happy family. Assuming this is a happy family?"

I nod. "For the most part, yes."

"You need some arguments in here. It looks like it's all sisters?"

"Well, one older brother and four younger sisters."

Gemma barks out a laugh. "Oh God. I can't imagine if that were our family. Mason would go absolutely mental."

"Considering how you and Ivy drove him crazy at the bar, I don't doubt that."

"That's what needs to be in this scene."

"A cranky older brother yelling at his younger sisters?"

Gemma smacks me on the chest. "No."

"What does the scene need then?"

"It needs more life. Anyone with a big family knows it's nothing like that. It's all shouting and laughing and more noise than you know what to do with."

"And where can I find some inspiration?"

Gemma taps a finger against her lips. "If only you knew someone with a big family."

"Are you suggesting a Winchester family dinner?"

"I am."

"Wouldn't that be weird to have an interloper there?"

Gemma's head tips back in laughter. They way her neck moves as she laughs is hypnotic. "You make it sound like I'm bringing a spy to dinner."

"I'm not going to lie; your grandpa intimidates me."

The few times I've seen him around the ranch, a cowboy hat blocked his face from view. It gives him the air of someone you don't want to mess with.

"Gramps? Please." Gemma pats me on the arm. "He's the nicest one of the bunch. You have to worry about Mason."

"That doesn't make me feel any better."

"What you did at the bar will go a long way to winning him over."

"That makes me more nervous than it should."

"Please?" Gemma clasps her hands together, turning pleading eyes on me. "They'd love to have you. I'd love for you to be there and meet my family."

"As long as you're sure I wouldn't be imposing."

"Not at all. Logan might be a bit cranky if he shows up."

"Cranky? You're not putting my mind at ease."

"He's only cranky because he can't play football anymore. It's really not his fault."

"So Mason might like me. Logan, who may or may not come, might be cranky. Peter seems to like me."

"He does like you. Nash too."

"Got it. Who else do I need to be worried about?"

With the few girlfriends I had, I never had to worry about impressing their families. As much as I hate to say it, the Travers name got me far. I could go in and be as interesting as a brick, and her parents would love me.

Considering no one in this town knows me, I can't skate by on my name alone. Not that I would want to.

I have an overwhelming urge to want to impress Gemma's family. I see the way she talks about them. There's nothing but love and adoration.

Quite the contrast to my family life being shuffled between nannies on movie sets.

"I promise, they are going to love you." There's a tenderness in her eyes that helps calm me down.

"As long as I don't ask Logan about football, or look at you like I know what you look like naked, I'm good?"

Gemma snorts. "You'll be perfectly fine."

"And if it's not?"

Gemma leans closer, her breath ghosting over my lips. "Then I'll think of a way to make you feel better."

I lean into her, wanting to take her back to my bed and have my way with her. "Think I can get an advance on the cheering up?"

But before I can kiss her, she leaps out of my hold. "Hold on to those thoughts, cowboy. I've got to get over to the lodge and get some stuff done."

"You're really going to leave me in distress all day?" I whine.

She nods and hops back to my room. "It'll make it better tonight, I promise."

I don't know how this woman plays me like a fiddle, but she does.

And I can't say that I don't love it.

Chapter Twenty

GEMMA

"Do I look okay?"

Blake smooths his hands over his chest. The flannel shirt stretches across his broad chest in a mouthwatering way. It's like his jeans were made for him. I can't resist keeping my hands on him.

"Do a spin for me." I wiggle my finger in a circle. He gives me an assessing eye before doing as I ask.

As expected, his ass looks perfect in those jeans.

"Oh, yeah. You're looking good, cowboy." Squeezing his ass, I smirk as he gives me a dirty smile over his shoulder.

"Am I just a piece of meat to you?" He laughs.

"Oh, no." I drop a kiss on the side of his neck. I love the cinnamon smell that seems to cling to every inch of him. I slide my hands around his waist, pulling him back into me. "So much more than that."

"Like what?"

"I don't know if we have enough time for that before dinner. And we don't want people to think we've been up to no good."

"You're killing me, Gemma."

"Remember what I said. After dinner."

I pat his chest and hop down off the porch.

"You're lucky my nerves are getting the best of me, otherwise I'd drag you back inside this cabin and have my way with you."

Flutters burst out of my stomach. Everything I'm feeling for Blake is new. I never felt like this with past boyfriends. It's fun and exciting.

I know I shouldn't get attached. Blake is only here for a few more weeks. But I can't help it. The more I'm with him, the more I want to be with him.

"We can't disappoint the Winchester family. Everyone is excited you're coming to dinner."

"They are?" Blake jogs to catch up, wrapping his arm around my shoulders. Our pace is easy as we set off toward Gramps's house.

"Mm-hmm. I told them all about our resident writer, and they want to meet you. We've never had someone like you here. Royalty, sure, but not a TV writer."

"Royalty?"

I smile up at him. "Story for another day."

"That's just giving me more ideas to work into my own."

The horses are running the pasture behind the barn as we get to the house. If the cars in the drive didn't tell me my siblings were here, it's the voices carrying outside that does it.

"Is it too late to turn back?" Blake's voice is quiet. Turning to face him, he looks more nervous than he did earlier.

"You work at big TV studios, and this family is scaring you?"

"Yes, because I—"

Whatever he was about to say gets cut off as Mason throws open the screen door.

"Thank God, you're here. I can't handle them anymore."

Mason drops a kiss on my head as he heads back the way we came.

"Where are you going?" I shout at his retreating form.

"Getting dinner from the restaurant."

"But it was your turn to cook."

"Don't start!" he hollers back.

"You remember Mason." I turn, giving a bigger than necessary smile to Blake.

"Is he always so happy?"

"He's a teddy bear. C'mon. I'll introduce you to everyone else."

Laughter greets us as we walk in the door. Layla is fussing over Logan as Willow comes racing over to me.

"Aunt Gemma! You brought Blake!" She leaps into my arms.

"You remember me." Blake is beaming at Willow, like she made his whole night.

She nods at him, her curls bouncing. "Of course I did! I thought of my favorite things during the storm and it worked!"

"Hey, that's awesome!"

"Did you have to think of your favorite things?" she asks him.

His eyes drift to mine, and I can't fight the smile that spreads across my face. "I had some of my favorite things, so it was even better."

"Cool!" Willow kisses my cheek and runs off.

"I'm one of your favorite things, huh?" I ask, giving Blake my best cocky grin.

"What can I say? I wasn't scared." He gives me a sweet peck on the lips.

It's then that I notice the house is quiet, which is unusual for this clan.

All eyes are on us as I turn to face them. Now it's not only Blake who is nervous, but me too.

"Who's this guy?" Logan asks from his spot on the couch. The cage surrounding his leg is covered up. Probably best that way. He had another surgery a few weeks ago to remove more damaged tissue. To say it looks gnarly is an understatement.

"Logan. Manners," Gramps barks at him from his spot in the chair.

"Sorry. Gemma, please introduce us to your guest." I can sense the sarcasm in Logan's tone.

I ignore him. "This is Blake. He's the one writing the family drama."

Layla walks over and introduces herself first. "It's nice to meet you. I'm Layla, Gem's big sister."

"Nice to meet you." Blake shakes her hand.

Thank you I mouth to her when she turns to me. She knows how much I like him.

"TV. What's that like?" I leave the two of them to talk, knowing he'll be in good hands with Layla. At least one person has their sanity tonight.

I stalk over to Peter. "Would you be nice?" I hiss at Peter.

"What have I done?" he whispers back to me.

"You're glaring. I like him, so *be nice*."

"Logan's the one being a dick."

"I heard that," he shoots back.

"What's got everyone in such a mood today?" I huff out.

"They want to be the big bad brothers and intimidate

Blake," Nash says, coming out of the kitchen, handing me a glass of wine.

Thank God for Nash and someone who isn't related to us having some common sense.

"You guys are di…jerks," I correct, seeing that Willow's looking right at me.

"Uncle Peter, you should be nice to Gemma's boyfriend. He's really nice and not scared of storms."

God, I love my niece, but the look that Peter throws my way could cut glass.

"Oh, he's your boyfriend now?"

"When I like a boy at school, that's what we call them," Willow states matter-of-factly.

"Why don't you go play in the backyard, sweetheart?"

Willow shakes her head. "Uncle Logan said we could play video games together."

Of course.

"Will you guys please be nice?" I plead again, not for the first time tonight.

Layla and Blake walk over to us. At least someone is cordial.

"We'll be the perfectly respectable people you know we can be," Peter states.

"Why does that not sound like the case?" Nash wraps an arm around Peter, kissing his cheek.

"Do you doubt we'd be anything different?"

"To mess with your sister? Yes."

I point at all of them. "I hope you remember this when you bring someone home."

"I already have my someone."

"Aww. Aren't you sweet?" Nash gives him another sickeningly sweet kiss.

"And you forget. I've already brought someone home.

Not doing that again." Layla glugs back the rest of her wine and heads back into the kitchen.

"Why did Mason rush out of here?"

I change the subject. No need to bring up my sister's painful divorce now.

"We gave him shit over not cooking dinner tonight. Said he had an issue at the bar."

"What issue at the bar required him to leave?"

"I don't know," Peter grumbles, sipping on his drink. "Everything was fine this morning. Something's up with him."

"Why do you say something's up with him?" I ask.

Blake is standing next to me, eyes ping-ponging back and forth between all of us.

"It's my bar. Don't you think I'd know if there was an issue? Something's up." Peter gives me a duh face.

"What's up with who?" Willow bounds into our little circle.

"Nothing." Peter looks properly chastised by the seven-year-old in the room. "We're talking about adult stuff."

"I hate adult stuff." She crosses her arms. "When is dinner gonna be ready? I'm hungry."

"Right now." Mason appears again, kicking the door shut behind him, two heavenly bags of food in hand.

"Yes!" Willow pumps her arm and runs to the table.

Nash and Peter go to help Logan get up as Layla finishes setting the table.

"You were right, by the way." Blake wraps a hand around my waist.

"About what?"

He grabs the wine glass out of my hand and finishes it. "My family dinner was crap. It's nothing like this."

I smile. "C'mon. Let's get you a drink. You haven't seen anything yet."

Grabbing the bottle of wine, I hand Blake a glass and top us off. Everyone is waiting for us at the table. His ringer is loud over the brief moment of silence.

Pulling it out of his pocket, he winces. "Sorry. I need to take this."

"Sure." I give him what I hope is a reassuring smile. He walks back into the empty kitchen as I take my seat.

"When was the last time you invited someone to family dinner?" Layla whispers, leaning across the table to get closer. Peter and Mason finish pouring the rest of the drinks.

"It's been a while."

I know exactly how long it's been. Since my high school boyfriend. Sure, if I was dating someone for more than a few weeks, they'd meet Layla or Ivy, but I never liked anyone enough to bring them around my family.

"You like him." Layla gives me a knowing look.

"Shh!" I look down the table, making sure my brothers are still occupied. The last thing I want is them *actually* drilling Blake tonight. "I know, so just let it go."

"Sorry about that," Blake says, taking the seat next to me.

Layla helps Willow pile mac and cheese on her plate, but not before casting a glance at Blake.

I turn my attention back to him, dropping a hand on his leg. "You're fine."

The smile he gives me in return doesn't quite reach his eyes. It sets off a flood of nerves in my stomach.

"Everything okay?"

"I'm real glad you could join us, Blake," Gramps interrupts.

Food is spread out on the old, wooden table. Chicken, steak, vegetables. Mac and cheese just for Willow. I don't know the last time I missed a family dinner.

It's one of the reasons I love this place. Our family history is etched into everything.

"Thank you for inviting me," Blake says, a little more at ease now. "Gemma told me my family dinner scene sucked, so I'm glad I can get the real deal."

"You told him that?" Layla asks from across the table. She passes the dumplings across the table.

"I said it much nicer than that."

"She did," Blake confirms. "I already know she was right."

"How'd you write this family dinner?" Mason asks.

"As Gemma said, not enough noise."

Everyone bursts out laughing.

"We are not that loud, Gem," Peter laughs.

"You want to think about that statement again?" Gramps gives Peter a stern eye.

"I'm the quietest one here!" he defends.

"Yet, whenever you get into a tizzy, you get louder and louder." Mason tosses a roll at Peter's head, where it bounces and rolls across the table.

"I thought you said we couldn't throw food?" Willow asks around a mouthful of orange noodles.

"You can't," Peter tells her, "but I can." He hefts it back at Mason who grabs it out of the air and takes a bite.

"So you agree then that you get louder as you get riled up?"

"I only get riled up because of you!" His voice grows louder, proving Mason's point. "Tell him I don't get riled up, Nash."

"You don't get riled up, dear." He drops a placating kiss on his cheek.

"Wow. See if I let you into the house tonight."

"I'll take you home, Nash," Logan tells him. "We can lock him out."

"That's it, I'm changing the locks." Peter stuffs a bite of chicken into his mouth as everyone continues to give him grief.

"Are all of your dinners like this?" Blake whispers.

"Yes. Sometimes, there's even a black eye."

"A black eye? I'm seriously beginning to think that I've been missing out all these years."

"I have three brothers. When they got really mad, punches were thrown, and then it was over."

"Damn." I see Blake's eyes taking in both of my brothers. Logan's built stockily like a football player, whereas Mason's arms are the size of my head and could scare even the biggest body builder. "I wouldn't want to take on either of them."

"Don't worry,"—I pat his cheek—"they don't really get into fights anymore."

"Although, we could if you hurt Gemma," Mason cuts in. Holding his knife in one hand, he points it at Blake. "Don't think we don't know what you're doing with our sister."

"Oh, shit," I hear Blake mumble.

"Oh, grow up, Mason. You don't know anything."

"I know a lot more than you think." He quirks a brow in my direction, giving me a fierce stare. One that used to have me caving like a sandcastle when we were little.

Not now. Not anymore. My big brother doesn't scare me.

"How about we ask where you were this afternoon?" I lean back in my chair, crossing my arms.

"Ooh, she's got you there," Logan laughs.

"I'm sorry if they're acting like children, Blake." Gramps gives Blake a warm smile. "They weren't raised in a barn."

"Can I be raised in a barn? I want to live with Buttercup!" Willow chirps.

Everyone bursts out laughing.

This is the reason I love my family. All of the jabs and bickering are done with love. I don't know how Blake did without this growing up. Even if I complain about being the youngest, I wouldn't trade it for the world.

"No living in the barn, sweetheart." Mason gazes down at Willow with affection. "You wouldn't like the smell."

"Then a tent maybe."

"You'd miss Daisy too much."

The mention of their dog has Willow thinking. "Daisy would come with me. She likes the horses."

"You bet she does," I tell her.

"Daddy would miss me though."

"I would, Pipsqueak."

"Maybe Aunt Gemma and I can have a sleepover with the horses. That'd be fun!"

"We'll see." I give her a wink and go back to my dinner as the table dissolves into more conversation.

"So, Blake." Gramps turns his attention to the man in question. "How much longer do you think you'll be staying here?"

"Haven't given it too much thought," he replies, shoving a forkful of chicken into his mouth.

This is something I haven't been thinking about. It's easy to forget that Blake hasn't always been here. It's like he was made to be by my side. The last few weeks have been sailing by too fast. And I know that he'll be leaving here soon enough.

Which is why I haven't been thinking about it. I've been enjoying what precious time I have with him. In and out of the bedroom.

"We've enjoyed having you here. I hope you'll come back again sometime."

"I'd like that."

Blake turns a happy smile to me. I know Gramps's words mean a lot to him, especially with how nervous he was.

Dinner is cleared and blackberry crisp is brought out.

With a big topping of light pink whipped cream.

"You think we got the preview last night?" This time, when Blake whispers, it's so only I can hear. Not that anyone can hear us as dessert is handed out.

"You two okay over there?" Layla asks, a knowing smirk on her face.

"We're just fine." I fight the laugh that threatens to burst from me. I turn my attention back to Blake. "We definitely got the preview last night."

"I don't think I can look at anyone if we eat that."

"I don't think I can eat it at all." My cheeks flush.

Layla hands two plates to us, piled high with blackberry crisp, a wistful look on her face. I know it's hard for her seeing happy couples.

Before I know it, dessert is over and people are starting to head home. Blake stands, grabbing my hand.

"I hope we didn't scare you off, Blake." Gramps extends his hand toward Blake.

It does funny things to my insides seeing the two of them together. Gramps is one of the most important people in my life.

We don't see our parents often, having retired to the warmer beaches of Florida. Sure, they were here when Logan was going through the worst of his recovery, but once I started working at the ranch, Gramps and I got closer.

He's the one person's approval I want more than anything.

"It was a great night. Thank you for having me."

"You're welcome back anytime. I mean that." Gramps points a finger at Blake.

Gramps turns to me, wrapping me in a tight hug. "He's a good one, Gem."

"Thanks." It's the only word I can get out.

This thing with Blake was supposed to be easy. Fun. The reckless thing to do.

I give him the true western experience, and he helps me fulfill my own…well, needs.

I didn't think twice about bringing him to family dinner. Now, things seem a lot deeper than I want to let on.

Chapter Twenty-One

GEMMA

"Are you ready to explore Dixon today?" I shout back to Blake in my bedroom. Ever since we started this thing, we've been spending more and more nights together.

Him teaching me everything he knows. Me experiencing pleasure I never thought possible.

"Ready."

Blake walks out of my room with a bright smile on his face. God, is he ever the sexiest man alive. I'd put his face all over magazines, but I want to keep that smile to myself.

"How are we getting into town?"

"Old Betty."

"Old Betty?"

Stepping outside, I point to the bright red truck. "She's Gramps's truck. Had her for thirty years."

Blake whistles. "Wow, she's pretty."

"He'd be happy to hear you say that."

"I mean, I know he likes me, but he still is kind of scary." Blake hops up into the passenger seat as I slide in on my side.

I laugh as I shift the truck into gear and head toward town, leaving the ranch in the rearview mirror.

"He's not scary."

Blake points his body toward me. "You can't tell what he's thinking with those bushy eyebrows of his."

Giving Blake a sly grin, I turn onto the main road. "I'm glad you got to meet him. He likes you."

"I need to write him into my show."

"Oh, yeah?"

The skies are gray as we head into town.

"Every good family drama has that paternal figurehead."

"And you want to base yours off Gramps?"

Blake swivels his head. "Yes and no. I don't want to make it exactly like him, but something like that."

"That doesn't really answer my question."

"Maybe the parents of the kids died and the grandparents raised them."

Dixon comes into view ahead, still plenty of road to cover before we get there. "I think you've got the drama part covered."

"Still a work in progress. But my producer liked what I sent him."

"Oh, yeah?"

"Says it's some of the most inspired writing he's seen from me."

"That's great, Blake." I peer at him from the corner of my eye. His face gives nothing away. "When do you think you'll know if they decide to start filming?"

"Not sure. Depends on how fast they want to move. Could be as little as a few weeks, maybe a few months."

The happiness from this morning slides away. I hate thinking about Blake leaving. His life is in LA. Mine's here.

We couldn't be more different if we tried.

Pulling into town, I find a spot and pull Old Betty in.

"Thank for coming with me today." Blake grabs my hand, linking it with his.

I push away the unwanted thoughts of Blake leaving and steer us toward the crowded park. "The farmers' market is the place to be on a Saturday."

Squat, brick buildings line the road. Flower boxes are bursting with color along the windows. Banners hanging from old gas-lit streetlights advertise the small market.

It's picturesque.

"Well, I'll be. You finally came to see us, Blake!"

Mrs. Reynolds rushes over to us in a flurry of bangles and oversized shawls.

"Umm, hi?" Blake has no idea who this is.

"Blake, this is Mrs. Reynolds. She's one of the piemakers here in town."

"One of? Gemma, have I taught you nothing? I'm the best piemaker in town. I'll show you."

She walks back to her table, grabbing a slice of her famous blueberry pie. She shoves it into Blake's hands. "The first slice is on the house. So you know what good pie is when Mrs. Phillips tries to convince you what's good."

"Oh! She brought pie over to me when I got here."

"Of course the ol' bat did," Mrs. Reynolds grumbles.

Blake takes a bite of pie, moans of happiness emanating from him. "I don't know, this pie might take number one."

"You hear that, Phyllis?" Mrs. Reynolds shouts across the field. "Man knows his pie!"

"Only because you shoved it in his face the minute they got here!" Mrs. Phillips shouts back. "He knows my pie I dropped off a few weeks back is even better."

Green eyes are bouncing back and forth between the

two women like it's the most entertaining thing he's ever witnessed. And he keeps shoveling bites of pie into his face.

"When you're done, Blakey, come on over here, and I'll remind you why my *real* pie is the best in town."

"Blakey?" the man being fought over says, swallowing the bite in his mouth.

"Told you you'd be a hot commodity." It's too tempting not to give him a peck on the cheek.

"Aren't you two just the cutest." Mrs. Reynolds is grinning like a fool at the two of us. "Blake, how long did you say you'd be in town?"

A quick look washes over his face, gone just as fast as it came. It's like he knows his time here is limited too.

"A few weeks. Plenty of time to come back and get some more pie."

Mrs. Reynolds waves him off. "What a schmoozer you are. I'm sending you two home with a pie to enjoy tonight. My treat."

"Oh, no." Blake sets his empty plate down. "I insist on paying for it."

"You'll break my heart if you don't take my pie."

"We can't have that, can we?"

Blake takes the pie being pressed into his hands.

"Now, go meet Dick." She shoos him off, but grabs my hand. "Gemma, dear."

"Yes, Mrs. Reynolds?"

"I hope you're taking advantage of that young man." She waggles her eyebrows at me.

"Mrs. Reynolds!" My mouth hangs open. I shouldn't expect anything less from her.

"Oh, don't look at me like that. My husband may have passed, but I still have eyes. And that young man is a tall drink of water you need to be drinking out of."

I have no doubt my cheeks are fire-engine red. "I will…take that under advisement."

"You do that, sweetheart. You do that." She winks and sends me on my way.

"All good over there?" Blake is waiting for me with a smile on his face.

"All good."

"Looking a little warm there, Gem."

"Stop it." I shove him in the direction we need to be walking.

"I'm starting to see why you love small towns so much."

"Not small towns. This small town."

"I'm glad I landed in Dixon." Blake wraps an around around me as we come up to Dick's table.

"Good. Now, meet Dick."

"Gemma! It's been a minute since I've seen you." Dick comes around his table and opens his arms to me.

"Hi, Dick." I wrap him in a hug.

"Wait, you're a real person?" Blake looks confused. "I thought Gemma was making you up."

I smile up at the man who is consuming my every thought. "Blake. Please meet Dick, otherwise known as Ghost Pepper Dick."

Dick's laugh is boisterous. "I forgot that's what you kids used to call me when you were little. Last time I ever gave you hot sauce to try."

"It's hard to forget when you try one of your ghost peppers because you think you're a badass."

Blake sticks his hand out. "Hi, Dick."

Dick eyes it with suspicion. "So you're the famous writer we've heard so much about?"

"Does everyone here know about me?"

Dick laughs. "Small-town gossip. People knew you were

here before you checked in at the ranch."

"Okay, then." Blake laughs. "Can I try some of this famous hot sauce I've heard so much about."

Crossing his arms, Dick eyes him up and down. "Tell you what. You put me in your show, and I'll give you all the free hot sauce you want."

Blake sticks his hand out for Dick to shake. "That sounds like a fair trade."

"Great. Now, you going to try the ghost pepper sauce?"

"Do I want to?"

"You'll be a true Dixonite if you do."

Blake hands the pie over for me to hold. "Then give me a sample."

Dick is beaming as he pours some hot sauce into a small, paper cup for Blake and hands him a carrot.

Blake takes a hearty bite, chewing before his face gets red. And redder. And redder.

"Holy shit!" He drops the cup and grabs the milk that Dick is holding out for him in his hand. "How do people eat that?"

"They don't." Dick is beside himself with laughter. "That's what we like to give unsuspecting tourists when they come into town."

Blake turns watery eyes on me. "You let me fall for that?"

"Oops?" I smile back at him. "If it makes you feel better, you're a true Dixonite now."

"You're only saying that to make me feel better."

Dick comes around the table, clapping Blake on the shoulder. "I only give it to the people I like. Welcome to Dixon, son."

Blake is beaming as he turns back to me. "Hear that, Gem? I'm a true Dixonite now."

If only.

Chapter Twenty-Two

BLAKE

"Horseback riding? Really?"

I give a hesitant look to the hulking animal in front of me. With a chestnut coat and a white diamond on her head, she's beautiful.

Doesn't make her any less terrifying.

"I will not make you do jumps." Gemma fixes the saddle, adjusting the…footholds? I have no idea what they're called.

"What if she throws me off?"

Gemma steps closer to me, placing a peck on my cheek before walking around the horse.

"Buttercup is our sweetest horse. Even the grumpiest of people do well with her."

"Are you telling me I'm grumpy?" I pout my lips at her.

"No. I'm saying that even those who hate horses love riding her. She's good to everyone." Gemma gives her an affectionate pat. "I promise, you'll be in excellent hands."

"Can't I just walk along beside you?"

I've lived in the city my entire life. It has never crossed my mind to ride a horse. It's a foreign concept to me.

"Your story will be terrible."

"What?" This time, I'm confused.

My story. The show. The whole reason I'm here in Dixon.

After getting the call from Clint during family dinner, the deadline of my time here is getting closer and closer.

I should be fucking ecstatic that the execs are loving my show. I am. But that means I'll need to be back in LA sooner than I want to be to start preproduction.

It's easy to picture the two of us doing this every weekend. Fishing. Riding horses. Spending our nights together.

Fuck. Growing up like I did, places never felt like home.

Gemma? I can see it so clearly with her. Making a home here in Dixon.

"You want horseback riding in your show, right?" She pulls me away from those dangerous thoughts.

I nod.

She beams up at me. "Then you need to get your ass up in the saddle and learn to do it. Make it authentic."

Gemma comes around to my side, keeping one hand on Buttercup.

"I'm really thinking I don't need horseback riding on my show."

"Wow. You go from wanting to fish on a horse to not wanting to be near them."

"I've never done this. Give me a break."

Gemma slides her hands around my waist. "I wouldn't take you somewhere if it was going to be a hazard to your safety. I promise."

Her eyes sparkle up at me. Damn. It's so easy to trust her. Dipping my lips down, I kiss her senseless.

"Mm." Gemma pulls back, swaying farther into me. "There will be more of that if you get on this horse."

"Alright, cowgirl. Show me how it's done."

"Grab here, foot in the stirrup, and then push up and swing your leg over."

She mimics what I need to do. I do it with far less grace than she does. After landing awkwardly in the saddle, my body stiffens up.

"How about we do a few laps around the barn? Would that make you feel better?"

"God, yes."

She smiles up at me. "Okay. Grab the reins and hold on to the horn,"—she puts my hands where they need to go—"and just relax."

"How long have you been doing this?"

Gemma leads, the path around the barn well worn.

"I've been riding for as long as I can remember."

"I honestly don't know if I've ever seen a horse that wasn't pulling a carriage somewhere."

"Really?" She looks up at me as we loop around the barn. It smells like horses and hay. It brings a smile to my face, remembering that first day with Gemma. To think we'd be here now.

"Really. When I tell you I'm a city boy, I'm a city boy. Mom likes the finer things in life. If she couldn't be flashy with her money, we didn't do it."

"You try steering now."

Gemma lets go of the reins and walks beside me. "Like this?" I hold up my hands and she nods.

"This really is your first time out in the country, then?"

"I don't know if I could have made it any more obvious."

Buttercup leads me around the ring with little guidance from me. The more we walk, the more comfortable I get.

"I wanted to be an Olympic equestrian when I was little."

"Why aren't you?" I flash my eyes down at her before looking back to the ring. Even if I'm doing nothing to guide the horse beneath, I don't want to lose focus.

"I was never good enough. I was competitive in high school, but I didn't have the drive that other riders had. All I wanted was to ride Buttercup and not worry about my next jump."

"Sounds like you had a good plan B."

"Have you always wanted to write?"

"For as long as I can remember. I used to make up stories and draw pictures to go with them when I was little. I called it Blake's Adventures."

"That sounds like the title of a really great documentary." She halts us. "Do you think you're ready to hit the trails?"

"As ready as I'll ever be."

"Great. Give me a minute."

Gemma walks over to where her horse is tied up and readies him with ease. She does everything with a grace I never thought possible. I must have looked like an idiot trying to get on this horse.

Gemma? Gemma looks as if she floats up and over as she settles onto her white horse.

"Let's go, cowboy."

It's like Gemma's voice is a beacon to Buttercup. She heads toward her immediately.

"You lead the way, cowgirl."

The trail outside the barn is wide, allowing us to walk side by side. The path is muddy after all the rain, but the sun is bright and warm. Gemma clicks at her horse, and we head toward the trees.

"Back to these adventures," Gemma says. "Where would you go?"

"Where would you want to go?" I throw the question back at her.

"I would love to visit my family in England. White sand beaches in Mexico. Eiffel Tower." She peers over at me. "Sounds pretty basic, right?"

"Not basic at all. It sounds pretty amazing."

It sounds pretty amazing because I'd love to do all of that with Gemma. I can picture it—her spread out on the beach in a tiny swimsuit. Me getting to rub sunscreen all over her.

"I wish I had more time off here." Her voice sounds wistful.

"Why don't you?"

Gemma leads us through the trees, where the path narrows. Buttercup falls into step behind her.

"I'm the only kid who works at the ranch. Everyone else is so busy with their lives that it feels hard to take time off. Like I'm abandoning the family. Even though Gramps doesn't seem to think I'm ready to take on more."

"I don't think that's how they think of it," I tell her.

"Don't get me wrong, I love what I do. But I want to experience more of the world than Dixon."

"Dixon's a pretty great place."

She smiles back at me. "It's the best place in the world."

"Complete with its own Ghost Pepper Dick."

Gemma tips her head back in laughter. She's in her element. I love getting to see her like this. "Something you will experience nowhere else in the world."

"I don't think anyone would believe me if I told them."

The trail gets steeper as the sun fades behind the trees. Rocks line the path we're following. It doesn't faze Gemma.

Me? I can't help but look down at how much narrower the trail is.

"It's fine."

I look up. Gemma is turned around, focusing on me. "What?"

"The trail. This is the easiest of our trails."

"That doesn't make me feel any better."

"Eyes on me."

I blow out a breath, focusing on the woman in front of me. A ball cap covers her head where a braid falls down her back. She's got a calm smile on her face.

"Shouldn't you be paying attention?"

She shakes her head. "Old Man River here knows the way."

"Is that really his name?"

She nods. "It was that or Trout. I didn't think he'd want to be named after a fish."

"Was he named after a river because he wanted to go fishing in it?"

Gemma barks out a laugh. "You really want to try fishing on a horse, don't you?"

"Of course I do!" I shout up to her as the trail curves upward. Fallen logs line the trail, making it seem more secure.

"I wouldn't even know how to start. There is no fishing on horses."

I pat Buttercup as she takes me farther up the mountain. "Maybe Buttercup and I will make a break for it. Head for the river." She tosses her head back at me.

Gemma points at her before spinning back around. "See? Even she knows that's a terrible idea."

"And here I was going to give you an acknowledgment in the credits. Guess you can forget about that."

Gemma's body shakes with laughter. "I should get that line because I'm making your show authentic."

The path levels out and widens. To the left of us, the

ranch stretches out below us. In the short time we've been out here, we covered a lot of ground.

Gemma pulls the horses to a stop as I move next to her.

"Okay, maybe not fishing on a horse. But this would make a good plan B."

Pushing her hat up, Gemma wipes the sweat from her brow. She's glistening. And looks fucking sexy as hell. I can't get over how gorgeous this woman is.

"Would it be redundant to say it's my favorite view?"

"I thought the hiking trail was?"

She shrugs a shoulder. "It is. And so is this."

"How often do you come out here?"

"I try to come out here with Buttercup at least once a week. She's great with guests, but I love getting to do the harder trails with her."

It's like she knows we're talking about her. She turns her attention to Gemma, who gives her an affectionate rub on the head.

"Yes, you're my girl," Gemma purrs at her.

"Do I get to be your guy?" I stick my face out toward her.

"Aww. Do you want me to rub your nose and give you carrots?"

"Please?" I jokingly ask her.

She rubs a finger over my nose. Grabbing it, I pull her in closer.

"Look who's getting more confident on a horse."

I lean in closer, a breath away from her lips. "I have a wonderful teacher."

"And you're an excellent student."

Tipping her hat up, I kiss her. Slow and sweet, until Old Man River starts to move.

"I guess someone doesn't like that," she laughs.

"Man, I've got some competition."

"Between you and the horse? Easy."

I quirk a brow up at her as Buttercup follows. She really is the best horse. "Why do I have a feeling you're talking about the horse?"

"I guess you'll have to catch up with me to find out!" she yells over her shoulder.

The rest of the ride is easy. Following Gemma is a no-brainer. Her laughter makes it effortless to focus on her and not on the trail as we descend.

Before I know it, the ranch and the barn are coming back into view. Gemma hops off her horse and then comes over to me.

"Swing your leg out and over, and then you can drop your other foot."

This time, my movements are less awkward. I hop off with ease, even though my ass is sore.

"Wow. Look at you."

"Am I a regular cowboy or what?"

"Just what I've always wanted. A cowboy."

"Maybe I can wear my hat for you?" I wrap my arms around her as the horses stand on either side of us.

"That cowboy hat is a good look for you, Blake."

There's a heated look in her eyes. Oh yeah, I'm liking this idea.

"Better get me a lasso then, so I can wrangle up my cowgirl."

"You think I'm getting caught up in your lasso?" Her hands drift under my T-shirt.

"Like you'd even try to resist."

"Maybe I should get you one. Test out your skills."

"You'd be surprised." I tilt her head up. "You'd make a pretty good catch."

"If I let you catch me." Her brown eyes are playful.

"I think I've already caught you."

And she's caught me. I don't know who is more caught up in this thing, but I'm falling fast. The very last thing I expected when I came here.

But this woman?

I'd let her lasso me up every day.

Chapter Twenty-Three

BLAKE

"Should it weird me out you're doing this?" Peter asks as he tosses me another pillow.

"I want to do something special for her."

"Did I really need to help?"

"Hey, you offered."

"I'm really starting to regret it."

"It's a date."

Peter groans. "And I know what happened the last time I took Old Betty out for a 'date.'"

Now I'm groaning. "I don't want to think about that."

I set the last pillow in place and admire our work.

Twinkle lights dangle from the cab of the truck. Pillows and blankets line the bed, and a cooler sits with food from the ranch and a bottle of wine. The last rays of the sun are peeking through the now-full trees.

It's cool, but not cold, on this spring night.

The perfect night for Gemma.

"I feel like this is where I'm supposed to do my big brother duty and ask what your intentions are with my sister."

I laugh. "No offense, Peter, but Gemma scares me way more than you do."

He rubs a finger over his brow. "She's never been one to take any shit from any of us."

"Who's bringing her up here?" I ask.

"I think she said Layla volunteered. Something about Ivy being busy tonight. Huh."

"Huh, what?" I turn to face him.

"Mason said he was busy tonight, so that's why I'm covering for him at the bar."

"You think something is up between the two of them?"

Headlights pass over us as a car appears at the end of the clearing.

"I'm going to take that as my cue to leave. Have fun tonight." Peter points a finger at me. "But not too much fun."

"Thanks." I nod at him as he leaves.

My nerves are high. I know Gemma will love this, but I hate that she's unsure about us.

I want to be with her. More than I've ever wanted to be with anyone else. The last few weeks have gone by in a blur. If I'm not spending time with Gemma, I'm writing in the ranch lobby.

Clint is eating up everything I'm sending to him. He loves it. The studio loves it.

I wish I could share in their excitement. I love what I'm writing, I really do.

But with each script sent to Clint, it's that much closer to me leaving Dixon.

And Gemma.

And that's not something I'm ready to think about.

"You summoned me?" Gemma appears between the trees and stops dead in her tracks. She looks fucking gorgeous, as usual. Her hair falls in curls around her shoulders and she's wearing a simple dress with flowers on it. Her cowboy boots and jean jacket complete the look.

Shocked eyes are focused on the truck, taking everything in.

"Surprise."

"Blake, this is…" Tears well in her eyes when she turns to face me. "This is incredible."

I close the distance between us, spearing a hand through her hair. "I wanted to do something special for you."

Her eyes keep straying to the truck. "It's something alright."

"Come check it out." I kiss her cheek before pulling back. Hopping up into the bed of the truck, I reach a hand down to pull her up.

The setting sun in the distance illuminates her. She couldn't look more perfect if she tried.

It has my heart stopping in my chest.

When I head back to LA, I don't know what I'm going to do without her.

"I really don't know what to say." Gemma sits down on the blankets, resting against the side of the truck.

"How about some wine?" I hold out a glass for her and pop the cork out of the chilled bottle.

"I won't say no to that."

I pour us each a glass and then take a seat next to her, not leaving any distance between the two of us.

"To us." She clinks her glass against mine and sips. My eyes stay trained on her neck as she swallows. Everything about this woman is pure grace.

"How'd you find out about this place?"

I hold out my hand for her, wanting the connection. She links her fingers with mine. "I asked Peter."

Gemma screws her face up. "Should it weird me out he helped plan this?"

I laugh. "He said the same thing. It's not like I could have found this place on my own."

"You would've found something, cowboy. You're blending in nicely."

I pump my fist in victory. "Does that mean I'm an honorary Dixonite?"

"Ghost Pepper Dick already crowned you one." Her eyes are playful.

"I think I might need a pepper badge to make it official."

"That,"—she points her glass in my direction—"will absolutely make you a true Dixonite."

"Does it count if I buy one myself?"

"I mean, you did buy yourself a cowboy hat." Gemma's smile is lively.

"And I look damn good in it." My hands pull her legs over my lap, running down over her knees and to her beat-up boots. "Just like you look pretty good in these, cowgirl."

Setting down her wine, Gemma straddles my waist. My hands immediately find her thighs, drifting over the exposed skin. I want to sink my teeth into all that soft skin. Hear the way she cries out at every nip and bite as I mark her skin. The way her dress rides up is almost indecent. The thought of what lies hidden below has me licking my lips.

"Thank you, Blake." She leans closer, a sparkle in her eyes. "This might be the most perfect date anyone has ever planned for me."

"Only for you, Gemma." I capture her mouth in a heated kiss. Her lips are cool from the wine. I drink in the taste of her as her tongue licks into my mouth.

I love how confident this woman is. She takes what she

wants without apology. I only wish she could see how incredible she is and ask for what she wants from her family.

When her fingers undo the buttons on my shirt, I lose all rational thought. Holding her close, I flip us over so she's on her back.

The lights reflect in her eyes. The glassiness is back. Whatever is passing between the two of us feels heavy. It's like Gemma knows I'm leaving and doesn't know what the future holds for us.

I know what I want it to be, but Gemma's life is here. Mine's in LA.

Instead of worrying about the future, I kiss her. I put everything I'm feeling into this kiss.

I want her to know how I cherish her. How I crave her. Desire her.

Love her.

Fuck.

I'm all in with this woman, and I can't pull myself back from the ledge. I've already gone over with no chance of rescue.

Her fingers tangle in my hair as I deepen the kiss. Each pass of her tongue over mine has my dick growing harder and harder. I settle between her legs, letting her feel what she does to me.

"Blake."

My hands drift under her dress, finding the cotton of her underwear already wet with need.

"Let me take care of this problem for you."

Cover from the trees blocks the moon. It's dark out here, the only light coming from the string of lights.

Pushing her dress up, I blow a breath over her pussy. Her moans are music to my ears. I drag a single finger over the material. Gemma continues to squirm.

I love knowing what amps up her desire.

"I can't wait to taste you, cowgirl." My tongue follows the path my finger took.

"Taste me." She's breathless with need.

Pulling the material aside, I lick her folds. Savor the taste of her on my tongue.

Her fingers find my hair, pulling tight. I slide a single digit inside her. She drenches my finger with her need.

"That feels so good."

"It's going to feel even better in a minute."

I lower my mouth, latching on to her clit. Gemma's body arches into my touch. I attack her pussy with the need I'm feeling.

Her need is palpable, like electricity flowing through the air. She takes everything I'm giving her. I ignore my growing need as I continue to flick her clit with my tongue, dragging a finger in and out of her.

"Keep going. I'm so close."

I chance a peek at her. Her head is thrown back in pleasure. She's strung tight, ready to explode.

"Come, Gemma."

It's a demand. I want her release all over me. I want it on my tongue as I fuck her into oblivion. I want everything this woman will give me.

"Blake!" Her scream echoes in the small space as her pussy squeezes my fingers, and I hold my face right there. I lap up every bit of her orgasm.

It seems endless. Peering up at her, she's boneless. An arm is thrown over her eyes as I move up her body.

"How was that?" I pull her arm down. Her eyes are closed, but a small smile plays on her lips.

"The best orgasm I've ever had."

I work open the buckle of my belt. "See, when I hear

that, I hear that the other orgasms I gave you were mediocre."

She opens one eye. "Not what I meant at all. But if you feel the need to keep giving me earth-shattering orgasms, I won't stop you."

"Has anyone ever told you how much sass you have?"

"All the time." Her hands trail down the opening of my shirt and meet my own. She does the rest of the work for me, pulling my cock out of my pants.

I drop my forehead to hers as her hands wrap around me and start stroking. Her touch is soft and light. As if she wants to hold me in her hand but not worry about getting off just yet.

I cover her hand with mine. "Are you trying to drive me crazy?"

"I was under the impression I already was."

"Fuck, Gemma."

I capture her lips again as I stroke our hands up my dick. I'm leaking everywhere. We're both greedy—me wanting more from Gemma, and Gemma sucking on my bottom lip.

"I never thought it'd be so hot to taste myself." Her breath ghosts over my lips.

"I'm happy to oblige anytime you'd like."

We're both mostly dressed, fooling around like teenagers in the back of a pickup truck.

Each roll of Gemma's hand over the crown of my cock has me closer to blowing my load.

"I need to be inside you." I release her and sit back on my heels. Grabbing my wallet, I pull out the condom and open it.

"May I?" Gemma pushes up onto her elbows.

I grin. "Abso-fucking-lutely."

She pulls the condom out and makes quite the show of

rolling it down my hard length. Her fingers trace the vein that's aching on the underside as she finishes her work.

"I want you to ride me, cowgirl."

I push my pants down to my ankles and settle against the back of the cab. Gemma hurries over me, taking my dick in hand and sinking down slowly.

Her skin is flushed as she takes me to the hilt.

Gripping the sides of my shirt, she swivels her hips.

"Fuck, Gem." I bite my lip, trying to stave off my release. I don't want to go too soon. I want to watch her take another release before taking me with her.

Leaning over, she slides her hands up my bare chest and holds on. Her movements are slow and controlled.

Each time she sinks back on me, she stills. It's like she knows it makes me crazy and keeps doing it.

"Gemma…"

"You feel so good like this. The way you hit so deep. Mmm."

"Fuck." I close the distance between us, burying my face in her chest. I nip and suck on the soft skin of her tits. It doesn't make her move any faster.

She takes her time. I meet her thrust for thrust.

I pull the top of her dress down, taking her nipple into my mouth.

"Gah!" Her moves falter and I take the chance to change positions. Laying her on the blankets, I start pumping hard and faster into her. I hitch her leg over my hip for better traction.

"Are you close?" I growl. I'm out of my mind with need. I need release. But not before Gemma comes again.

She doesn't answer. Her pussy strangles my dick to within an inch of its life as she starts to come.

It only takes a few more thrusts before I'm emptying myself into the condom.

"Fuck."

I'm dizzy with how hard my release slams into me. Nothing has ever felt as good as this. I don't know if it's because it's Gemma, or that I'm getting ready to leave, but I don't think anything will ever compare to this.

Gemma looks absolutely wrecked. One tit is hanging out of her dress, and it's all pushed up around her waist. Red marks line her chest from where I attacked it with bites and sucks.

I rest my body on top of hers. Her breaths are coming fast as my hand drifts up and down all that soft skin.

"That was incredible." Her fingers play with my hair. Between that and the orgasm, it's enough to send me into a blissed-out coma.

"Fucking amazing," I whisper into her chest. "Was that everything you wanted a pickup truck hookup to be?"

"Everything and more." I feel her laugh everywhere. "How was your first time in the bed of a pickup?"

I still her wandering hand over my heart.

"Everything and more."

Chapter Twenty-Four

BLAKE

"And here I thought a cattle drive would be more exciting."

"Were you planning on showing off those expert lasso skills?" Gemma asks, wrapping her arm around me.

"It got me you, didn't it?" I squeeze her closer to me.

"Pretty sure I came before the lasso skills. Otherwise…"

"Ouch. The real feelings come out." I step back from her, mocking a pout. "Guess I'm just going to go sit in my cabin all by myself."

Gemma grabs the lapels of my coat and pulls me back into her. My back collides with the side of the lodge.

"You will do no such thing, Blake Travers."

There's a fierce need growing in her eyes.

"Oh, I won't, won't I?"

My hands find her hips, squeezing, pulling her closer.

"Not unless it's with me."

Gemma tips her head up. Her lips are shiny, begging to be kissed.

"I guess I could spare some time for you." I tuck a loose strand of silky hair behind her ear.

"How big of you." Those brown eyes of hers are playful. I could write an entire scene on how much I love them.

Grasping her chin, I hold her close as I take what she's offering. Her soft whimpers have me deepening the kiss. I lick into her mouth, loving how responsive she is to me. Each swipe has me growing harder with need. Each lick has Gemma pushing closer to me.

Our need is palpable. The air around us thickens. I could stand here and kiss Gemma for hours and it wouldn't be enough.

"Blake! I've been looking everywhere for you."

A voice I recognize breaks me out of my lusty fog.

Clint. The very last person I expected to be standing on the porch right now.

"What the hell are you doing here?"

"I can ask you the same thing."

With a cravat on under his velvet jacket, Clint couldn't look more out of place.

"Why are you here?"

Gemma's gaze flits back and forth between the two of us.

"I come bearing good news from the studio."

"Shit, really?"

"Yes. Do you have a moment to talk?"

He studies the two of us. Gemma looks kissed to within an inch of her life.

"I'll see you later." Her voice, normally so full of joy, is quiet.

I track her as she passes Clint without a glance and disappears inside.

Fuck.

Scrubbing a hand down my face, I meet Clint at the bottom of the stairs and lead him to my cabin.

"What's this good news?" I don't beat around the bush, blurting out the question the moment we're inside.

"They love it and are ready to start."

"Wait, really?" I can't hide the shock from my voice.

"A family drama in a small western town? The execs were drooling for more."

"Wow."

"This place"—Clint looks around—"really did you some good."

Not just this place.

Gemma.

I don't think she realizes how much she helped pull my head out of my ass that day we went hiking.

I know Clint wouldn't be standing here telling me how good the initial drafts are without her.

"Next steps?" I lean back against the couch. Clint's eyes are taking in the cabin.

"Since we're late for pilot season, they're thinking of launching it on the streaming platform this fall."

"Really?"

That's fast even by Hollywood's standards.

"Really. They're impressed and don't want to wait. Whispers are that it's some of your best work to date."

"Even better than *Pirates*?"

Clint nods. "Even better than *Pirates*. They've got high hopes for this show."

"Okay. I'm assuming that means we'll start casting in a few weeks?"

"Monday," Clint corrects.

"I'm sorry, Monday? As in two days from now?"

"Do you have better things going on?"

"Well, no, not exactly."

Clint hooks a thumb behind him. "I'm guessing it has to do with that woman back there?"

My jaw grinds at the way he casually mentions Gemma.

"Look,"—Clint throws his hands up in defense and takes a step toward me—"I'm glad this place has been so good to you, but your life is back in LA."

"Do you think I don't know that?" I retort.

"Good. Then our flights are leaving tomorrow night. Studio wants to meet on Sunday to go over logistics."

"You can't push it back any?"

Clint shakes his head. "You know how things work."

"So we're leaving tomorrow."

"Tomorrow." Clint goes to leave, but turns around at the last minute. "Think I can get a room here?"

"They'll set you up."

I don't even look at him as the door clicks shut behind him.

A sinking feeling settles over me.

Not even thirty minutes ago, I was on a high, watching cows roam in their pastures as Gemma told me everything she loved about the land.

I could listen to her talk for hours. It's probably why the studio loved the script so much. So much of the love Gemma feels for this place was infused into it.

They way she talked about the ranch? She made it easy to write.

And now, instead of getting to spend the next few weeks with her, I'll be packing up and leaving her behind.

A soft knock at the door pulls me out of my spiral. Gemma's head pops in.

"I saw him leave and wanted to come see you."

Fucking Gemma Winchester. Always worrying more

about others than herself. She really is too fucking good for me.

"That was my producer."

I hold out my hand for her to take. She comes willingly.

"What'd he want?" Gemma steps between my legs. It's how we were standing earlier. Except this time, her fingers are playing with the buttons on my shirt. Her eyes aren't focused on me.

"The studio loved my script."

"Yeah?" That perks her head up. "I knew they would."

I cup her cheek, brushing my thumb along the apple of her cheek. "How could they not when I had Dixon to inspire me?"

"I mean, we are a pretty great place."

"The best," I correct.

"So they loved it. What happens next?"

I blow out a breath. I'm not ready to leave. I figured I had a few more weeks here at least.

I rip the Band-Aid off. "I leave tomorrow."

"You what?" Gemma's eyes meet mine. Tears gather there.

"Casting, rewrites…it all starts Monday."

"Wow." Gemma pulls back, hugging her arms over her chest. "So that's it?"

I don't expect the finality in her words. What I expect even less is how it feels like a punch to the gut.

I grab her, pulling her into me. "It doesn't have to be."

"How, Blake?" There's a waver in her voice. I can't stand it. "I live here. You live in LA."

"Come with me." I don't think, I just blurt it out.

"What?"

"There are plenty of places you could work in California."

"Blake, I—"

"I'm serious, Gemma. You could do so much more than you're doing here. People would be lucky to have you."

It was the wrong thing to say, because Gemma's eyes harden. "Just because I'm not doing what I want here doesn't mean I'm not happy."

"But are you?" I fire back.

"What kind of question is that? Of course I am. I'm working at my family's ranch. It's all I've ever wanted to do."

"What happened to the girl wanting more?"

"I can still be happy."

"So that's it?"

"Why don't you move here?"

"What?"

"You seem to think it's so easy. Why can't you move here?"

I spear a hand through my hair. "My entire life is in LA. I can't write TV shows from here."

"And I can't run the ranch from LA."

I go to her, taking her hands in mine. "It doesn't have to be the ranch. Don't you see how incredible you are?"

"But I can't leave, Blake. Don't you get it? I'm the only one here to help."

"You can hire someone."

"It's not the same thing. This is a family-run ranch, and I don't want to turn it over to some person who won't love it like I do."

"Nothing I say is going to make you change your mind?"

A lone tear slips down Gemma's face. "I think we were kidding ourselves if we ever thought we could make this work."

"I really don't want to leave," I confess.

"I don't want you to leave." At the break in her voice, I pull her into my arms.

Soft, sweet Gemma.

Sassy, sexy Gemma.

My cowgirl.

The person I've fallen for.

Fuck.

I don't know how it happened, but I'm head over heels for this woman. The one who just turned me down.

"We still have tomorrow," I whisper.

"Won't that only make it harder?"

She's right. Fuck, I know she's right. But right now? I'm greedy. I want every single second I can get with her.

I don't want the last time I see her to be a fight over who should move where.

I want to slide inside her heat one last time. To remember every stitch of pleasure etched onto her face. To hear her cries and gasps. To feel her fingers digging into me, urging me on.

I want it all.

"I don't care. I want you, Gemma. More than I've ever wanted anyone before."

Gemma steps back, linking her hand in mine. She doesn't take those sad brown eyes off of me as she leads me back into my bedroom.

Our kisses are slow. We take our time with each other. Licking and savoring the other's body.

We put everything we're feeling into this last time. Every ounce of sadness and pleasure and love. It's all mingling together as we come together.

And when I wake up in the morning?

She's gone.

Taking my heart with her.

Chapter Twenty-Five

GEMMA

"Thanks again for covering."

"No sweat."

I hand over the iPad filled with the new arriving guests and walk over to the bar. Ducking under the counter, I grab a bottle of wine and head to Gramps's house.

My feet carry me along the well-known path. It's not until I'm passing Blake's cabin that I stop.

It's been two weeks. Two weeks since he left, and I can't walk by his cabin without wanting to fall into a puddle of tears.

Everyone has been telling me it'll be okay and I'll move on. No matter how many times I try to tell them to leave me be, they want to fix the problem.

I rush past his cabin and arrive at Gramps's at the same time as Mason and Willow.

Mason looks about as miserable as I do.

"What—"

He doesn't even let me get the question out. "Don't start, Gemma."

He stalks off toward the house as Willow grabs my hand and pulls me down to her level.

"Daddy's really sad."

"Do you know why?"

She shakes her head, tiny curls bouncing. "No."

"Then how do you know he's sad?"

"Whenever Daddy is sad, I get to watch extra cartoons."

Kids. Always so in tune with everyone else's emotions.

"Maybe Daddy just needs some of Aunt Layla's mac and cheese."

She holds my hand and walks inside. "Aunt Layla doesn't know how to make anything else, does she?"

"Shh. We like to let her think that she's better at it than she is."

Willow's giggles help calm the raging emotions inside of me.

"Why do you two look like you're up to something?" Peter grabs the bottle of wine from me and heads into the kitchen.

"Nothing!" Willow gives him a guilty look.

"There's my little Pipsqueak!" Gramps comes into the room and holds his arms out for Willow. She goes running.

"Hi Gramps!"

"How are you?" Layla wraps an arm around my waist and steers me into the kitchen.

"I'm fine."

Her blue eyes study me. I hate how intuitive my older sister is. It's one of the reasons I've steered clear of her these last few weeks. I don't want to open my heart and make it bleed anymore.

"Then set the table." She pushes a stack of plates and silverware into my hands. "Dinner's ready."

"I just got here." Dinner is never ready on time.

"And you were late. So was Mason." She shoos me into the dining room. "And don't think I haven't noticed that he's been grumpy too."

"I don't know anything about that." I set each place setting with a little more force than necessary.

Peter and Nash are pouring the drinks. The only person missing is Logan.

"Is Logan not coming to dinner?" I ask Nash.

"No. He said he wasn't feeling up to it."

"I'll take him a plate later," Layla says. "Willow, do you want to go with me?"

She shakes her head. "I don't want to. Uncle Logan was grumpy the last time I saw him."

The way her lip quivers has my heart breaking. Out of all of us, she's taking his change in mood the hardest. After his last surgery, he had a small setback. Nothing major, but it sent him spiraling. And he took it out on anyone who came to see him.

"It's okay, sweetheart." Mason rubs her back. "You and I can get ice cream on the way home. How does that sound?"

Her face lights up. "Sprinkles too?"

"Sprinkles too."

The mention of sprinkles has the pieces of my heart cracking. It was the day Blake spent with us making sundaes.

Why do I have to miss him so much? He was never mine to take.

Mason brings dinner out. It's a quieter affair than normal. More subdued. The clinking of forks against plates is loud in the room.

"You okay?" Layla nudges me from the side.

"I'm fine."

"You don't sound fine," Mason chimes in from his side of the table. His arms are crossed, giving me a fierce look.

"Why are you so concerned?"

"I can't be concerned about my little sister?"

"Mason, leave her alone." Layla comes to my defense.

"Why are you getting mad at me?" He throws his arms up in defense.

"Because I don't want to talk about it!" I explode.

"Fine. Then I won't ask again." He stands, going to grab Willow's plate.

"I'm not done yet!" She grabs the plate back. "Go be grumpy with Uncle Logan, Daddy."

"Fine." He storms off into the kitchen, the door swinging shut behind him.

"Okay, is it something in the water? Because first you and now Mason is stomping around." Peter waggles a finger between my brother and me.

"Leave me alone, Peter." I don't want to be the center of attention right now.

"You've been sad ever since Blake left. I didn't think he meant that much to you."

His words cut deep, snapping what little control I have left.

"Thanks, Peter. I'm sorry if I'm not all sunshine and rainbows right now. I'm sad because the man I was in love with left!" I yell. "I'm sorry I can't just bounce back and be fine, but I'm miserable because he meant so much more to me than you could ever imagine."

Five sets of eyes stare back at me.

"That's a lot to digest," Gramps says.

Willow hops up from the table and wraps me in a hug. "I'm sorry your friend left and made you sad, Aunt Gemma. I still love you."

"I love you too." I hug her back, my voice watery.

Embarrassment burns hot on my face as I stare at my family. I don't think any of them expected that outburst from me.

I'm always the one to take things in stride, but for once, I can't handle it.

"Come outside with me, Gem." Gramps holds his hand out, and as much as I want to protest, I don't. Following him to the porch, I drop into the rocking chair next to him.

"I'm sorry for snapping like that."

"I've had a broken heart once before too," Gramps tells me.

"You did?" Tears are welling in my eyes. Now that I snapped, all my emotions are brimming just under the surface.

"Your Gran broke up with me when I went away to college. Said I didn't care about her enough to want to stay."

"What?" This isn't something I've ever heard before.

He nods, pulling out his pipe and lighting it. "Miserable that whole first year. I loved my Peg something fierce, and it hurt like hell."

"It really does."

I thought I knew what heartbreak was when my high school boyfriend cheated on me. Apparently that was nothing compared to this.

"It's like someone ripped your heart out and stomped all over it."

I laugh, dry and humorless. "Pretty much."

"Do you love him?" Gramps asks.

I nod. "I really do."

"Would you want to move to LA? Think about it. Really think about it."

I shake my head. "I don't have to. My life is here. I love this place and don't want to leave."

"You don't?" Gramps turns a confused look to me.

"I don't know why you sound surprised. The ranch. Dixon. My family. This is what I want in life."

"You surprise me, Gemma. Always have. You've always kept us on our toes. I thought you were just biding your time until someone swept you off your feet and took you far away from here."

"You did?" This time, I'm giving him the confused look. "When have I ever said I wanted to leave here?"

"You didn't. I made a poor assumption. You've always had dreams, and I guess I thought they'd take you away from this place."

"Gramps." I reach out, grabbing his arm. He blows out a puff of smoke. "This place has always been my dream. Why do you think I've fought you so hard to be the one to run the place?"

"I'm ashamed to say I didn't want to give you the position because I didn't want to lose you. Not just from the ranch, but from my daily life as my granddaughter. I always thought you were meant for bigger and better things."

"You really thought I'd leave?"

He nods.

"Gramps, I love you and I love this place. There is no getting rid of me."

He stands, holding his hand out to me. I take it as he wraps his arms around me. The smell of tobacco is heavy. It's comforting. It reminds me of every time I had a skinned knee when I was little and he was there to make it better.

"Then I think it's about time I made it official."

"What?"

"Manager. You want to run this place?"

I pull back, wiping the leaking tears from my eyes. "Are you serious?"

"It's yours."

Tears fall unchecked as I wrap my arms back around Gramps. "Thank you."

"I should be telling you I'm sorry. I just wish you didn't have to get your heart broken."

"It really sucks." Now that the tears have started, I don't know if I'll get them to stop.

"Love is never easy."

"I wish it were."

"But if Blake loves you like I suspect he does, you two will find your way."

If only.

Chapter Twenty-Six

BLAKE

The lapping of the waves against the shore pulls me out of my restless sleep. The last few days have been a blur. With the studio approving the first drafts of the script and casting underway, they want to shoot the pilot to send it out to interested buyers for streaming rights.

It's been a lot of long nights finalizing it in order to start scouting potential locations today.

The loud chirping of my phone cuts through the empty bedroom.

"Hello?" My voice is gravelly.

"You ready to start casting today?" Clint's voice booms through the line.

"How long have you been awake?" I rub the sleep from my eyes.

The sounds of the city waking up filter through my open window.

"Since five." A knock sounds on my door. "Now come let me in."

Fuck.

It's too early to deal with anyone, let alone Clint when

he's in a good mood. And that's always on a day when we start filming.

I drag myself out of bed, throwing on the first pair of sweats I find. I didn't do a single goddamn thing yesterday.

Is this what it feels like to have your heart ripped from your chest?

Because if so, no TV show writer has ever gotten it right before. It's a million times worse than they show.

Unlocking the door, my eyes lock onto Clint's. I don't miss the way he looks over my appearance.

"You look like shit." He hands me a cup of coffee and walks inside.

"Nice to see you too."

"We've got a lot to do this morning. Are you going to be up for it?"

I suck back half my coffee in one gulp, nearly singeing my tongue. "I'll be fine."

"Are you going to shave?"

I run a hand through the scruff on my jaw. "Do you really think they'll care if I'm not clean shaven?"

"No, but I do. What's wrong?"

I ignore him, walking out to the balcony that overlooks the beach and dropping onto the cushioned chair.

"You going to ignore me?"

"Trying to." I laugh, sucking down more of my coffee. At least it's making me feel more human.

"Is this about that girl?"

"That girl's name is Gemma," I growl. He says it so casually that it grates on what few remaining nerves I have.

"Of course this is about her." He laughs. "I don't think I've ever seen you so sad as you were before we flew home on Sunday."

"Sorry I'm not more chipper."

"Look, Blake. Clearly Dixon meant a lot to you. But

today is a big day. This show could mean big things for you, and I don't want you to mess it up because you're sad."

"Are you fucking kidding me right now?" I roar. Whatever thread I had on my sanity has snapped. "I'm sorry I'm not living up to whatever image you have in your head of me, but you'll get what you get today."

Clint gives me a no bullshit look. It's one he's used often with me.

And one that I don't always like.

"You love her."

I grind my jaw together, shifting my attention back to the beach.

Surfers are out riding the waves. People run by on the boardwalk. A couple walks by on the sidewalk holding hands.

And I'm sitting here with a broken heart.

"I do."

"Think she'll come here?"

I shake my head. "Her life is in Dixon."

"Maybe it wouldn't have worked out."

"Are you serious with this shit, Clint? I'm barely holding on as it is."

"Hear me out."

"Fine." I settle back in my chair, kicking my bare feet up on the balcony railing.

"I once moved for someone and it didn't work out. I thought we were so in love that we were going to get married and have kids and live that two-point-five-kids, picket-fence life."

Dread swirls in my gut.

"After a while, we started to resent each other. I resented her for making me move, and she resented me because I wasn't the same person after I moved. Sure, it hurts now, but maybe you saved yourself some heartache in the long run."

I blow out a breath. "But what if we didn't? What if she's the person I'm supposed to be with?"

"If you're really supposed to be together, then you'll find your way back to one another."

This gets a laugh out of me. "That's really glass half-full kind of stuff from you."

Clint stands. "What can I say? I'm a sap. It brought me here and I found the actual love of my life."

"And here I thought I was the light of your life."

"You test me in more ways than I ever thought possible, and I know this week is going to be hard for you. But at least try, okay? For me?"

I stand, clapping him on the shoulder. "I'll do you one better. I'll even shave for you."

"Wow. I guess I should wait until after then to give you the bad news."

I groan as I head back inside. "What's the bad news?"

"Your mom wants to be the matriarch in the show."

"Please tell me you're joking."

"She seems to think that she has some sway with the studio because of the writer."

"Fuck me. This is the last thing I need to deal with today."

"Then don't. Let me handle it, and you just worry about yourself. And that beard."

Clint. At least he's good for something.

<hr>

"THIS IS YOUR IDEA OF MOUNTAINS?"

I throw my hand up to shield the sun from my eyes. Spring has made its way to SoCal.

"You wanted it to be authentic, right?" Clint's tone is patronizing. "What's more real than mountains?"

"Clint. These look like ant hills. No one is going to believe we're in Wyoming."

"Use your imagination. It'll be fine when we shoot."

"And the number of cars zooming by? Will that be okay when we film?"

"They have people there, right? It'll be fine."

"Not this many."

Nothing about this place feels right. The mountains aren't really mountains. There are too many people. Not enough trees.

It doesn't give me the vibe I want for my show.

The vibe of Dixon.

"I'm a fucking idiot." I slap my hand across my forehead.

"What's going on?" Clint comes back over to me.

"Why aren't we shooting on location?"

"What?" He looks confused.

"I mean, why are we shooting a western drama in Malibu?"

"Because we live and work here…"

"I'm serious." I shove my sunglasses on top of my head. "Why aren't we shooting this where there are mountains and fields and actual horses?"

"Money?"

"You said our budget was fine. Was that wrong?"

"Well, no. I'm just trying to think of a reason it wouldn't work, but I'm coming up empty."

A smile grows on my face. "Why the hell didn't I think of this before?"

"Because everything you've ever done has been in LA?" Clint asks, tongue in cheek.

"But we could shoot on location?"

I don't want to get my hopes up. I know permits can be difficult to come by in some areas, and don't want to walk too far down this road if it won't happen.

"I can float it by the execs."

"You do that. And while you're at it, show them those pictures you took of these 'mountains.'" I throw up air quotes.

Clint rolls his eyes at me. "I get it. You're a badass western kid now who knows what a real mountain looks like."

"I can even ride a horse." I wink at him.

"I'm assuming you have a location in mind?"

I nod. "Do I ever."

"Will you stop moping around if we do this?"

"Hey. I haven't been moping."

"You're the definition of moping."

Clutching Clint's shoulders, I look him dead in the eye. "I promise, if we shoot there, I will be the happiest person on the planet and keep you in scripts for years."

"You promise?"

"What's a better motivation than love?"

Chapter Twenty-Seven

GEMMA

"Everyone have their schedules for the day?" I look around the small conference room at my newly hired team.

Nods are given as the meeting adjourns for the morning.

It's been two weeks since Gramps officially gave me the position. Two weeks of hiring a few new staff members to help run the front of the house. Of moving people into positions that they want to be in and hiring help for our new western camp I created.

It's not even the start of the summer busy season, and we're booked through the end of the year.

Word of mouth travels fast in this business, and we've been lucky. Everyone from town is telling me how happy the guests are when they head into town.

I've been lucky.

I think one of the main reasons I never pushed too hard for this is because I didn't want to fail. I didn't want to disappoint my grandfather. He would never admit that to me, but I hold myself to a higher standard.

I love this place. It's in my soul. The reason I couldn't take off willy-nilly to follow a boy across the country.

Even though we've started seeing success, I don't want to settle. It could easily all go away with one bad review by an unhappy guest.

Following everyone out of the lobby, the family I've been working with is waiting near the barn.

"Hi, West family!" I greet the parents and two daughters.

"Morning, Gemma. We can't tell you how excited we are for today."

"We've got a great day planned for you. You'll be horse-back riding this morning followed by a picnic lunch before coming back to the ranch. You and your husband will have spa treatments this afternoon while your daughters will have activities with the other kids at the main lodge."

"That sounds wonderful," the mother tells me. "I know the girls will be so excited to get some time on their own."

I give her a warm smile. "It's one of the many reasons we designed the program like we did. Give the parents some time on their own and let the kids have some fun with the other kids on the ranch."

"Thank you." She shakes my hand and then follows her family toward the pasture.

I can see their excitement from here as Buttercup comes up to the fence. The girls are giggling away as she nudges their extended hands.

I know the smile on my face is sad as I head back toward my office. Every win, every bit of happiness I've felt these last few weeks has always come with an added weight.

The weight of a broken heart. It's been there since I left Blake in his cabin that morning.

I couldn't face him. I couldn't say goodbye. Because if I saw him that day, I wouldn't have been able to let him leave. He's everything I want in life, if only he weren't a thousand miles away.

And then I wouldn't be here at the ranch. In the position I once dreamed of having. Getting to put my mark on the place I love so much. The place that's branded into my soul. I could never leave here.

Some days are easier than others. Most days, I'm busy from sunup to sundown and have hardly a moment to spare a thought as to who isn't here with me. It's the moments like right now, when I can slow down, that my mind wanders to what could have been.

If only.

If only Blake didn't live in LA.

If only I didn't live here.

If, if, if.

It's not going to do me any good thinking about him. Of trying to move on.

"Gemma. We have a pretty upset guest out in the lobby. Would you be able to come talk them down?" our newest hire asks as she pops her head into my office.

"What happened?" I blow out a breath.

Is it too much to ask for one minute to myself this morning? The stack of paperwork on my desk keeps piling up with no end in sight.

"Something is wrong with their cabin and they wanted to speak to the manager. Well, with you."

"They asked for me by name?" That can't be good.

The lobby is empty as we leave the back office space. "Where are they?"

"Right here."

I stop in my tracks. I have to be imagining it. Brought it

to life by sheer force of will with how much I've been missing him.

Because there's no way that voice would be here. Not when it's supposed to be in LA.

Spinning on my heel, the man that I've been craving—missing like a limb—these last few weeks is there, leaning against the fireplace.

He looks scruffier than I remember. A beard fills out his face, hiding the smile that I love.

But those green eyes of his? Those are exactly as I remember.

"I need to register a complaint."

"You came an awfully long way for that."

Blake pushes off the hearth and comes closer to me. Each step has nerves gathering low in my belly.

"I'm gone for a few weeks and my desk is gone?"

My eyes lock onto the corner that is now desk-free.

"I didn't think it belonged there anymore."

"And why's that, Gemma?"

God, the way he says my name. I've missed it.

"It looked out of place without a writer."

"You missed me?"

I can't see the dimple with the beard on his face, but I know it's there with that blazing smile he sends my way.

I hold up my thumb and index finger, hardly any space between. "A little."

"Only a little?"

"A lot, actually." A voice comes from behind.

Swinging my head around, Peter is standing behind the desk with a knowing smile on his face.

"When did you get here?" I hiss.

He smiles back at me. "About the same time as Blake."

I turn my attention to my brother. "Were you in on this?"

"Someone had to get me here," Blake says.

"Let's go somewhere more private."

"What, I don't get to see what happens?"

Ignoring Peter, I grab Blake by the arm and drag him through the lobby and out of the lodge.

I'm not paying attention to where we're going, but the next thing I know, my feet have carried us to the barn.

"You're not going to try and dump more horse shit on me again, are you?" Blake takes a single step back, out of my reach.

My face scrunches up, trying not to laugh. "Not today, no. What are you doing here?"

"It's not obvious?" He quirks a brow at me.

"I mean, I get that you're here. But why? For how long?"

A million questions start firing through my head.

He's here. Seeing him, seeing that face that I love so much, settled all the aching, tender parts of my heart.

But for how long? I don't want to get my hopes up if he's here visiting. My heart couldn't take that.

"Turns out you can't film a western show at the beach."

Oh. The hope that filled me at seeing him rushes out of me. He's filming the show here.

"You'll be here for a few weeks then?"

He shakes his head. "No."

"How long then?"

"For good, if you'll have me."

"What about your job?"

Blake steps into my space. I forgot how all-consuming this man is.

"*Teton Grand* is going to take up a lot of my time for the next few months. And if it goes well, which we think it will, then a few years."

"Years?" My voice shakes.

"Years. I might have to travel a bit from time to time, but I want to make Dixon home."

"You do?"

Oh God, Gemma. Can you not string together more than two words? The man who has taken up almost every thought of mine over these last few weeks is here and it's like I forgot how to speak.

"How else am I going to make sure Ghost Pepper Dick gets a cameo in the show?"

Laughter burbles out of me. "I can't believe he asked you that! You do not have to put his hot sauce in the show."

"Oh no." Blake's arms come around my waist. "Not just his hot sauce, Gem. Him. People will love him."

"Any other people from town you expect to have in the show?"

"I'm sure Mrs. Phillips and Mrs. Reynolds will angle the producers for a spot, too."

"That's all?"

Blake's eyes focus on me. I feel his stare everywhere.

And I mean *everywhere.*

"Are you trying to see if you're in the show?"

"Maybe." I shrug a shoulder.

"I'll tell you more about the show later, but no, no role for you."

"What? You have parts—"

A finger to my lips shushes any argument.

"You're not in it because I don't want to share you. Not even a small piece of you with the rest of the world."

"Blake..."

"Let me finish."

I nod, letting him go on.

"I love you, Gemma. And these last few weeks, I was

absolutely miserable without you. And I know these next few weeks are going to be crazy with filming starting, but I want to be here in Dixon. With you. I want to go to the farmers' market on Saturdays and buy pies and *not* get tricked into trying hot sauce, and ride Buttercup. Kiss the fish."

"Will you really kiss the fish this time?" My voice is watery as tears are now rolling down my face.

Blake closes the remaining distance between the two of us. "As long as I get to kiss you after? Oh, yeah, I'll kiss the fish."

And then he kisses me.

Long and deep. With each pass of his tongue, it strikes the match of desire inside of me. The scratch of his beard against my face has my toes curling in my boots.

This is it. This is what I was always waiting for.

A man like Blake.

No one before him was worthy of having me.

All too soon, his movements slow and he pulls back. Half-masted eyelids stare down at me, pupils wide with need.

"I can't believe you're here." My fingers have a mind of their own, playing with his beard.

"I'm pretty sure Clint would have sent me back here in a week because he was getting sick of my pouting."

"You missed me that much?"

Blake lifts me into his arms and backs me against the side of the barn. "So much that it physically hurt."

"I'm glad I wasn't alone."

"You missed me too?" Blake asks, a sheepish look coming over his face.

I nod. "I kept telling myself that it was just sex between us, but it was a lie."

Blake nods, burying his face into my neck. His lips ghost over the soft skin there.

"It was never going to be just sex with us, Gemma. I told myself that I was doing you a favor as much as you were doing me one. But that first night?"

I pull his face up, wanting to see him when I tell him this.

"I'm glad I waited. Because it brought me to you."

"Does it make me sound like a caveman that I'm happy no other man will ever experience that part of you? That it's only me?" There's a growl to his voice.

I should hate it. It's not the reason I was waiting. But God, do I love that this man will be the only person I ever share that part of me with.

"I guess it was yours to take all along."

Chapter Twenty-Eight

GEMMA - TWO MONTHS LATER

"It's weird to be nervous, right?"

"I mean, technically you're not in it, so why would you be nervous?" Ivy stands next to me, surveying the scene in front of us.

Cameras are spread out throughout the pasture. Buttercup and Old Man River are standing near the fence with the actors.

It's Blake's first day of shooting *Teton Grand*. When he mentioned them shooting at the ranch, I thought it would be some background shots.

Instead, they're using the fields and the cabins for a large portion of shooting.

Bright blue skies. Snow-capped mountains. Wildflowers as far as the eye can see.

Every bit of it is stunning. And I know it's going to look gorgeous on camera.

"I want the ranch to look good. This could mean really good things for us."

It's something I planned on when negotiating the rate for shooting here. One of my first big duties as manager.

I was ecstatic, even if I was nervous as hell. Sitting across from Blake and negotiating a rate wasn't what I expected. The pride emanating from him that day made me realize we made the right decision.

"Gemma. Look around us. They couldn't have picked a better spot if they tried."

"Quiet on set!" Eric barks out. Blake looks every bit the professional writer that he is, sitting in his chair as he watches filming start.

He looks every bit the western hunk now. A full face of scruff. Plaid shirt opened over a white tee that stretches across his chest. Cowboy boots hiding under his jeans.

I absolutely want to jump his bones. Something that we do every chance we get now that Blake is living with me.

The scene unfolds before us. The Grand family has one older brother and four younger sisters. I'm not sure which sister this is that's filming, but it's her high school boyfriend that's breaking up with her. Something about wanting bigger and better things.

The actress is pouring everything into this scene. She's a new up-and-comer, and I can't wait to see what she does with this show.

"Cut! That was brilliant!" Eric shouts.

He's also someone I've gotten to know over the last few months. He's been a permanent fixture at the ranch since we started scouting locations.

It's nice that Blake has people here outside of me. His mom is not one of them. Eric managed to score her a part in a period drama that is currently filming in England. The one time I met her, she intimidated the crap out of me.

I should have known I didn't have to worry about Blake not having people here. Blake makes friends everywhere he goes, as evidenced by the fact that Blake and Eric go out with Dick every Thursday night. I love that he's making this place his home.

"How's it look from over there?" Blake drops his headphones and walks over to us. Sweeping me into his arms, he lays one on me.

I don't think I'll ever get used to this.

"It looks fucking awesome," Ivy tells him. "Seriously. I can't wait to see the show."

"Thanks, Ivy. How's school going?"

A sad look washes over her face. "It's going."

Ever since she moved to Montana, it's been hard on her. She came home for the weekend for the first day of shooting, but she won't tell me what's wrong.

And I hate it.

I don't pester her about it. It only upsets her more.

"I'm going to go grab a drink. Do you guys want anything?"

"I'm good," Blake and I answer at the same time.

"God. You two are disgustingly cute." She rolls her eyes and stalks off.

"You hear that?" Blake wraps his arms around me and pulls me in close. "Disgustingly cute."

"Only the first time today." I capture his lips in a kiss.

"Then we might need to up the ante."

Blake goes back in for another kiss, his tongue sweeping into my mouth.

Every time he kisses me like this, it leaves me in a lustful fog.

"Blake. We need you back."

"Gemma, computer is down. We could use your help with check-in."

Voices yell at both of us.

Blake tucks a lock of hair behind my ear. "A manager's work is never done."

"And I guess you need to go make sure they aren't destroying your words."

"I'll see you for dinner tonight?" Blake whispers into my ear.

"Absolutely, cowboy." I slap his ass as I push him away. "Knock 'em dead."

He tips a fake hat in my direction. "Anything you say, cowgirl."

BLAKE

"AND HERE I thought I'd be the one running late tonight."

Gemma looks exhausted as she collapses onto the couch next to me. I've been reviewing scenes for tomorrow's shoot. "By the time we got the computer working again, it froze up. We'll need a new one before ski season starts."

"You've got your work cut out for you." I hand her a glass of wine and drop a kiss on her forehead.

"How'd the rest of shooting go today?"

"We got the one shot in and that was it."

"Really? You were out there for hours."

I roll my eyes. "Clint said they weren't putting enough emotion into it."

"Really?" Gemma takes a long pull of the red wine. "It was breaking my heart watching the two of them break up."

"I'll be sure to convey the message to him tomorrow."

I pull Gemma into my arms. A sigh of release escapes

my lips. It's only been twelve hours since I last held her, but it was twelve hours too long.

I've only been living here for the last two months, but I can't imagine anything different. It was a lot of back and forth in the beginning, moving out of my mom's condo and doing the preproduction in LA.

Within a week of landing in Dixon, we've been going nonstop. Locations, casting, you name it. I wanted to do it all here so I wouldn't have to be apart from Gemma. Time with her has been limited, so I take every minute I can get.

"You'll still get Sunday off, right?" Gemma wiggles in closer to my side.

"Just you and me."

It's the one promise we made to each other. With Gemma taking on more work now, and a grueling schedule of filming ahead, we wanted to make time for each other. A day with no interruptions. Just the two of us.

"Think we can get Buttercup and Old Man River away for a few hours for a ride? Do some fishing?" I ask.

Gemma bursts out laughing, her body vibrating next to mine.

"Am I going to have to take you fishing on horseback to prove you can't do it?"

"Maybe I can write it into our show and it'll be research to show what not to do."

"That's why you want to do it?" Gemma's hand comes down on my chest. It sends heat pulsing through me.

"If it gets you to do it? Yes."

"Only if you teach me how to surf."

"We'll only be in LA for a weekend, Gem. I don't think there will be enough time."

"Then you can kiss horse-fishing goodbye."

I laugh. "Is that what we're going to call it now?"

"Does it sound as dumb as you make it out to be?"

"Ouch. Way to crush a man's spirit."

Setting down her wine, Gemma slides over my lap, a leg on each side. "I'm sorry, cowboy. Do you need me to kiss it and make it better?"

"Yes," I pout, not in the least bit upset with Gemma.

"Where do I need to kiss?"

"Here." I tap my cheek. Gemma's lips are warm as she presses them there.

They move to my other cheek. Her mouth covers my face in warm kisses before finally landing where I really want them.

Gemma's brown eyes soften as she kisses me. It's unhurried. Languid. Like every time she wants to learn something new about me from kissing me.

I'll never get tired of her. This woman keeps me on my toes every day. It's never boring with her. She rocks over me, my dick already straining to be inside her.

Fuck. I'm greedy for her in every way.

I love that I have all of her firsts. That she'll have all of my lasts. The last thing I ever expected when I came to Dixon to get away was to find love.

That's exactly what I found with Gemma.

More than a story.

More than securing my future as a writer.

Gemma. The person I want to spend every minute with.

"Mmm. I like you making fun of me if it ends like this."

"Is that a blanket invitation to keep doing so then?" Gemma's lips are swollen.

"For you, cowgirl? Anything."

Epilogue

"Blake! We're going to be late." I huff out a breath, shoving my feet into my cowboy boots.

"Gemma. The show doesn't start for two hours. I promise, we won't be late."

I peek down at my watch. "It starts in an hour, Blake."

Opening the bathroom door, he walks out in a puff of steam. A towel sits low on his waist, his glorious abs on full display. Now I'm starting to question whether we really need to be there on time. Not when Blake looks like Adonis.

"See something you like?" He struts over to where I'm sitting on the bed, stepping between my legs.

"You know I do." My voice is deep and full of need.

He leans over, his lips hovering over mine. I tip my head up, wanting to close the gap.

"I guess it'll have to wait. Someone tells me we're going to be late."

"Ugh. You're mean." I throw myself back on the bed as Blake walks over to the dresser and pulls out a pair of black boxer briefs.

"Maybe if you weren't shouting at me that we're going to be late…" Blake drops the towel, throwing it at me.

"It's your big night." I pull it off my face. "I want everything to be perfect for you."

I watch as he gets dressed, stepping into a pair of jeans, and then walks back over to me. He kneels before me, sliding his hands along my thighs.

"You know tonight is already going to be perfect, right? You'll be there with me to celebrate."

I drag a finger along the bow in his lips, taking in the perfect structure of his handsome face. Some days, I still have to pinch myself that this is real. That Blake gave up his life in LA to move here and film his show.

Sure, there's a lot of back and forth travel during edits, but the fact that he's here? I couldn't ask for anything more.

And tonight is the big premiere of his show, *Teton Grand*. With it being filmed here, the studio wanted a big party to celebrate. I was at Peter's bar all day helping to set up for the after party.

"I know, I know. I'm worrying for no reason. I just want everything to be perfect for you." I link my fingers behind his neck, pulling him close. "You've worked so hard and I want everyone to love the show like I do."

"I don't think anyone could love it more than you, Gem."

"A family drama based here in Dixon? What's not to love?" I laugh.

Blake leans in this time, capturing my lips in a heated kiss. Even after all this time together, it sends my heart soaring and toes curling in my boots.

Blake pulls back too soon. "Listen, tonight is going to be crazy, and I want to give you something before we go."

Grabbing my hand, he leads me into the living room.

"Close your eyes."

"Really?" I quirk a brow at him.

"Do you want your surprise or not?"

"Fine."

I close my eyes as Blake guides me to the couch.

"Keep them closed." I hear a rustling noise before Blake takes my hand and presses something into it. "Open them."

Blake, now in a simple black T-shirt, is sitting on the coffee table in front of me. The package in my hands is a small box, complete with a big pink bow.

Pulling the lid off, I find a small book sitting on a bed of tissue paper.

The title?

Our Story.

"Blake…" My eyes are watery as I pull the book out and open it to the first page.

It starts with Blake arriving in Dixon. I turn each page, greedy for the next. I know this story. Lived every minute of it with him, but it's like I'm reliving everything for the first time.

Including… "Oh God, the horse shit. I still can't believe I ran into you."

"Thank God you did."

"I can't believe you made this."

"Keep reading."

His hand is on my knee, tapping out a nervous rhythm. The first hike together. The storm. Our fishing trip. Every moment of our love story plays out on these pages.

To the very end.

Where there's a little picture of Blake down on one knee in front of me.

My breath catches in my throat, eyes flying up to meet his.

"What do you think?" He has an anxious look on his face.

I smile back at him. "Three stars."

Blake goes from anxious to confused in the blink of an eye. "Three stars? Really?"

"I didn't actually hear a proposal…"

"Oh, you want a real proposal?" Blake asks, his dimple popping out. "I think I can give you that."

Blake stands, grabbing an even smaller black box from his pocket before taking a knee.

Every single nerve is buzzing as he takes my hand in his.

"From the very first moment I met you, I knew you were different. You've helped me in ways I never thought possible. You are one of the kindest, most genuine people I've ever met, and I don't ever want to be apart from you. I'm never happier than when I'm here with you, and if you'll let me, I'll spend my entire life trying to do the same for you."

Tears are falling down my face as Blake pops open the box. A simple, round diamond sits on a gold band. It's beautiful.

"You, Gemma Winchester, are the single greatest thing that was ever happened to me. Will you marry me?"

He barely says the words before I'm throwing my arms around him. "Yes! Of course, yes!"

Strong arms wrap around me. Blake buries his face in my neck, dropping kisses along my shoulder.

"Thank God. I about had a panic attack when I asked your grandpa and your brothers."

"And you're still breathing?" I laugh.

Blake nods, shifting me so I'm sitting on his knee.

"Do you know how terrifying they can be?"

"I'm sure they were perfectly reasonable when you asked them."

"Now that I'll be part of the family, I'm sure they will be."

Cupping his face, I take his lips in a kiss to end all kisses. A happiness I never knew I could feel fills the air around us.

All those years I spent waiting for someone to take my virginity, I thought I was waiting for the right person. Turns out, I was just waiting for Blake.

The perfect person for me.

Grabbing my hands, Blake pulls my left hand to his, sliding the ring down my finger. A perfect fit.

"It's gorgeous."

Blake kisses the ring. "Care to rethink that review now?"

"Five stars."

"Oh, yeah?" He leans in for a kiss. "That good?"

"Best book I've ever read."

THE END

Read on for a special bonus scene of Blake and Gemma working through her list…

Bonus Scene

BLAKE

"How long are you going to make me wait, Gem?" I stare up at the ceiling of our bedroom, still waiting on the woman I love.

"Have you always been this impatient?" Her voice is muffled from the bathroom.

"When you tell me you have a surprise for me? Yes."

"Patience, Blake. I'll be out in a minute."

A smile pulls my mouth up into a smile. Just a few short months ago, I never thought this would be my life. Shooting the new show here in Dixon has been the best decision I ever made. Because it brought me back to the woman I'm waiting on.

Shooting every day and coming home to Gemma has been everything. She keeps me on my toes. I'm still learning from her as much as she is learning from me.

It's why I love being with her.

"Ready?"

My gaze shifts to the bathroom door. "Hell yes."

Gemma steps out of the bathroom in a complete cowgirl costume. Her hair is down in two pigtails with a hat resting on her head. She's wearing a tiny vest that makes her tits look ripe for the taking. Jeans hug every curve of her legs.

"Holy shit."

She's never looked sexier.

My dick is immediately hard.

"You like?" She drags a finger down her cleavage. I'm fucking jealous of that tiny finger of hers. I want to push my face between them and ravage them.

"What's the reason for this?"

Gemma walks over to me, a sway to her hips. I sit up, scooting to the end of the bed.

"Ever since you moved here, we haven't really been working on my list."

"Are you complaining about the sex?" I quirk a brow up at her, running my hands over her thighs as she steps between mine. I want to tear these jeans from her body.

"Do you hear me complaining?" Gemma grasps my chin between her fingers and tilts my eyes to her, redirecting my focus to her.

"No."

"And I'm not. But I thought it would be fun to revisit it."

My mind goes back to that first morning we spent together. After I took her virginity. When she showed me her list of what she wanted to try.

Fuck. I love Gemma more than I ever thought possible.

A grin lights up my face. "Are you going to ride me, cowgirl?"

Her smile matches mine. "You know it, cowboy."

Grasping the back of my shirt, I pull it over my head. I don't miss the way her eyes track over my newly exposed abs.

"Lay back."

I obey, willing my dick to calm down. The minute she stepped out of the bathroom, he was ready to get in on the action.

Wasting no time, Gemma undoes the buttons on her vest. Each inch of skin that is exposed has my mouth watering.

Her fingers are deft, stopping just before revealing what I really want to see.

"Fuck." My voice is a growl. "Why'd you stop?"

My dick is screaming at me.

Gemma comes over to the bed, hopping up and straddling me. "Can't have it be over too fast."

Her lips come down on mine in a heated kiss. My hands fly to her waist, wanting to feel all her skin against mine. Her tongue demands entrance and I give it to her.

This is one of my favorite things. How good it feels to kiss her. My fingers dig into her skin, pulling her closer. Her denim-clad pussy grinds against my dick, driving me wild.

"Can you lose this now?" I drag my finger down her chest, finding the last button.

"I thought I was in charge?" Gemma whispers against my lips before tugging my bottom lip between her teeth.

Fuck. "When you look like a walking wet dream, can you blame me?"

"Hmm, maybe I can put you out of misery."

Gemma pushes up, undoing the last button and tossing the vest to the side. Her nipples are hard.

"So sexy. So damn sexy." I can't help leaning up and pulling one between my teeth. I don't get far before she's pushing me back and standing.

"Not so fast. Lose the pants."

It should embarrass me by how fast I lose my pants and

boxer briefs, but I don't care. Gemma is smiling from her spot.

"Someone's in a hurry."

"Can you blame me when you look like that?" I wave a hand in front of her. I sound like a pouty teen, but I don't care.

Gemma strips out of her jeans, throwing them to the side before stepping into a pair of cowboy boots I notice now at the end of the bed.

In nothing but boots and a hat, she is fucking stunning.

"You are the sexiest woman I've ever seen."

Taking my dick in hand, I give it a slow stroke.

"Not so fast, Mr. Tavers."

Gemma stops me, placing her hand over mine. I release my grip and let her take over.

Her mouth and hand work in tandem. Each swirl of her tongue around the head has me leaking into her mouth. She takes it all as she takes me to the back of her throat.

"Damn, that feels amazing."

The wet heat of her mouth has my balls tightening. The ends of her braids brush against my thighs, making it that much harder to not come down her throat.

As much as I want that, I'd much rather be coming inside her.

"Fuck, Gem. I'm close."

Pulling off me with a pop, Gemma wipes her lips. Swollen from sucking me off.

"Well, we can't have that, can we?"

Gemma moves over me again, rubbing her wet pussy over my hard length. Grabbing her ass, I guide her.

It feels so good to be sliding through her like this.

Taking me in hand, Gemma sinks down onto my cock, slow inch by slow inch. With the hat on, she's a vision.

Absolute perfection. I could write an endless show about her, but I won't. She's mine.

Only mine. No one else gets her.

"Fuck." I'm right there, thanks to all of Gemma's teasing.

"You feel so good inside me."

My hands drift up her legs, finding her slick clit. I strum it with each roll of her hips. Her pussy is a vise, squeezing my dick.

"So good, Blake."

Gemma's pace quickens. Her hands play with her hard nipples.

"Sexiest fucking cowgirl ever."

I thrust up into her each time she sinks down onto me. Her hips roll easily, working me over. Slow and tortured moves as she takes her own pleasure from me.

"I need you to come, Blake."

"Not without you, cowgirl."

Sitting up, I bury my face between her tits, licking and sucking on the tender skin there.

With each swivel of her hips, she's squeezing me even tighter. She's right there.

As I am.

Taking a nipple between my teeth, I tug it before licking away the sting.

It pushes Gemma over the edge, taking me with her.

"Yes!" Her shouts echo around the tiny bedroom.

"Fuck."

I breathe in her sweet scent as we come together. Unloading inside of her.

Every time, I feel like a man possessed. She takes over every part of me, and I willingly give it. I love this woman and how she makes me feel more than life itself.

Taking the hat off her head, I toss it away with our

clothes and pull her into my arms. Our skin is slick with sweat.

"How was the ride, cowgirl?"

Gemma smiles against my chest, pressing a kiss to my pen. "Best one yet. Why does it always feel so good?"

"Because we're amazing together."

It's not a lie. It's never felt this good before. I love getting every part of Gemma. Something no other man has ever experienced. And never will.

This woman is it for me. I love everything about her. That even though we're complete opposites, we work.

I wouldn't want to be anywhere else than here with this woman, thoroughly fucked and worn out.

"You know, if I recall, we're nearing the end of your list."

Gemma shifts, resting her chin on my chest. Her brown eyes are hazy.

"I believe we are."

"Maybe we could add to it."

"You have any ideas?" She traces a finger around my pec.

"What don't I want to do?"

It's like every single thing I want to do with her explodes in my mind. Every dirty thing we could do with each other.

We just finished, but I want round two. Now.

Gemma pats my chest. "Better get writing then, cowboy. I want it to be good."

I smile at those words I told her when we first started this thing.

"Good. You'll get it all."

Author's Note

Book 13 is out in the world!

I am so excited to be delving into this brand new world! Dixon was inspired by a trip I took with my friends in 2020 and my family in the summer of 2021. We visited a ranch in Montana and had absolutely the best time! I fell in love with the area near the Tetons we stayed, and so the two merged to form Dixon Creek. **If you're related to me and made it this far…yay! I knew you guys would love me writing, but also, I don't need to know you read my books, okay??

I've been laying the hints for this series…first in Royal Reckoning, and then again in the Denver Mountain Lions. My first ideas of this book are so different from those original notes. I love seeing how this world has evolved since then!

There are so many amazing author friends that have come into my life since I started this journey. Swati MH…one of the best people to have in your corner and is someone who will cheer you on from afar! Lily Miller…you always put a smile on my face and I'm so happy our paths crossed! For Claire and Suzanne…I'm so lucky to have you in my circle! To Katie…one of my OG author friends and whom I just love! To my book bestie Tina…thanks for making me laugh on a daily basis! The Ann's…for causing existential crises and making my books the best they can be! All my sprinting friends…Stephanie Rose, CE Johnson, Jess Bryant…I wouldn't have finished this book without you! I am beyond lucky to have so many wonderful people in my corner and thank you to each and everyone of you!

Thank you to my beta reader Jodi for making this book amazing! I'm so happy to have you on this journey with me. Thank you to every person that has read, reviewed, shared, created edits, TikToked…you name it, your support has been the best part of this journey. To my Street Team for your excitement for my books always puts a smile on my face! And my Travelers…my groups is my favorite little corner of the internet!

And to all the readers…I hope you love this new world I've built as much as I do! Your support means the world to me!

<3 Emily

About the Author

After winning a Young Author's Award in second grade, Emily Silver was destined to be a writer. She loves writing strong heroines and the swoony men who fall for them.

A lover of all things romance, Emily started writing books set in her favorite places around the world. As an avid traveler, she's been to all seven continents and sailed around the globe.

When she's not writing, Emily can be found sipping cocktails on her porch, reading all the romance she can get her hands on and planning her next big adventure!

Find her on social media to stay up to date on all her adventures and upcoming releases!

Also by Emily Silver

The Denver Mountain Lions

Roughing The Kicker

Pass Interference

Sideline Infraction

Illegal Contact

The Big Game

Dixon Creek Ranch

Yours to Take

Yours to Hold - coming June 29, 2023

Yours to Be - coming fall, 2023

Yours to Forget - coming winter, 2023

Off the Deep End — A standalone, MM sports romance

The Ainsworth Royals

Royal Reckoning

Reckless Royal

Royal Relations

Royal Roots

Royal Ties

The Love Abroad Series

An Icy Infatuation

A French Fling

A Sydney Surprise

Read all my books here: